Mourning Has Broken

A.S.Chambers

This edition published in 2024.
First published 2018 by Basilisk Books
Copyright © 2024 Basilisk Books.

A.S.Chambers asserts his moral right to be identified as the author of this
work.

Cover art © 2018 Liam Shaw.

ISBN: 978-1-915679-41-3

Acknowledgements

Many thanks to the extremely talented Liam Shaw for bringing the antagonist of Orion's Child to life in his stunning artwork.

Also, many thanks as always, to Theresa Hughes for being my ardent hunter of inaccuracies, misspellings and erroneous commas.

Also by A.S.Chambers

Sam Spallucci Series.
The Casebook of Sam Spallucci – 2012
Sam Spallucci: Ghosts From The Past – 2014
Sam Spallucci: Shadows of Lancaster – 2016
Sam Spallucci: The Case of The Belligerent Bard – 2016
Sam Spallucci: Dark Justice – 2018
Sam Spallucci: Troubled Souls – 2020
Sam Spallucci: Bloodline - Prologues & Epilogue – 2021
Sam Spallucci: Bloodline – 2021
Sam Spallucci: Fury of the Fallen – 2022
Sam Spallucci: The Case of The Pillaging Pirates – 2023
Sam Spallucci: Lux Æterna – Due 2024

Short Story Anthologies.
Oh Taste And See – 2014
All Things Dark And Dangerous – 2015
Let All Mortal Flesh – 2016
Hide Not Thou Thy Face – 2020
If Ye Loathe Me – 2022
Out of the Depths – 2023
Hear My Scare – Due 2025

Ebook short stories.
High Moon - 2013
Girls Just Wanna Have Fun – 2013
Needs Must - 2019

Novellas.
Songbird – 2019
Bobby Normal and The Eternal Talisman – 2021
Bobby Normal and the Virtuous Man – 2021
Bobby Normal and the Children of Cain – 2022
Bobby Normal and the Children of Cain – 2022
Bobby Normal and The Fallen – 2023
Bobby Normal and the Black Dragon – 2024
Child of Light – Due 2024
Child of Fire – Due 2025

Omnibuses.
Children of Cain - 2019
Macabre Collection: Volume One – 2022
Macabre Collection: Volume Two – 2023
Sam Spallucci Omnibus: Volume One – 2022
Sam Spallucci Omnibus: Volume Two – 2024
The Adventures of Bobby Normal – 2024

Contents

Orion's Child   1

Somebody's Gotta Do It   13

Frank's Castle   19

Not-So-Lucky Larson   23

Here There Be Dragons   38

TV Dinner   50

Wicked Intentions   51

Little Acts Of Kindness   58

Memento   66

Author's Notes   89

About The Author   95

Orion's Child

The moon hung full in the sky.

Pale light flickered over the hunter's muscular form as he prowled across the deserted moorland.

I have to stop thinking in cliché: Dootson thought to himself. *Spending too much time reading pulp novels.*

He yawned and ran his long tongue over his sharp fangs. Damn, he was tired. Full moon, the height of the month, and he had about as much drive as a Fiat Punto. In an attempt to rouse himself, he shook his head vigorously from side to side, causing his tawny-coloured fur to fluff up.

About as much use as an overweight Labrador: he sighed internally. As he padded across the open field, the peaty ground stuck to his paws. *That's gonna take a hell of a cleaning later. Typical.*

Life for Chris Dootson was, to put it simply, rather bleak. When he'd been turned into a werewolf a few months back, he had seen it as a way to up his social standing, rather like being in the Freemasons. He had wanted to join that bunch for some years now but, hey ho, no one had offered him a chance to wear a pinny and roll

1

up his trouser leg. Consequently, he had written it off as a no go, assuming that they were more into bank managers and lawyers rather than television aerial repairmen. Then, when he had found out about another secret society, the Bloodline of Abel, he had been all ears, especially when it brought with it super powers.

He had been all, *where do I sign?* Plus, there were no antisocial meetings to slip out to, so the missus didn't have to think he was up to no good. Although, come to think of it, she hadn't been that impressed at him saying he'd started watching certain astronomical phenomena once a month out in the middle of nowhere through his badass telescope. He had played the "light pollution" card and claimed that he needed to get out in the Trough of Bowland where the sky was so much clearer.

She seemed to have gone with it eventually, but when he skulked back home in the morning, there was always that atmosphere of "*you've been up to no good, haven't you?*" hanging over the breakfast table.

Yeah, he was going to have to keep an eye on that situation.

His front right paw sank into something unmentionable.

He was also going to have to keep an eye on where he was walking.

The unfortunate werewolf sighed, pulled his paw out of the cow pat and wiped it on the coarse grass. This was just about right, it really was. He had been promised so much. He had been told that the Bloodline was this worldwide organisation that lurked in the shadows of everyday life. His creator had been full of how they were inserted into positions of power around the globe. Wealth and riches would follow, alongside the supernatural powers he had inherited.

Chris considered that the only thing his creator had been full of was the shit that he had shovelled for a living. That was before he gotten himself gobbled up by a horde of driver ants.

Ouch. That had to have stung.

It certainly hurt for Chris. He was now left on his own with no mentor. He could hardly just Google, "I'm a member of a werewolf cult, what do I do?" That would really screw with his computer's browser history.

No, for the last two full moons he had been out here on his own. Not that Hawkins, his creator, had ever hunted with him. He didn't even think the guy had told anyone that he'd created a protégé.

So Chris just came out here once a month, changed into a wolf and wandered round the fields looking up at the night sky.

Carefully selecting a cow-pat-free area of grass, Chris lowered his rear down into a comfortable sitting position and looked up at his beloved starscape. As he did, he felt all tension and fatigue start to drain from his aching limbs. Yes, you really knew where you stood with the night sky. His hyper-keen eyes scanned the mythological figures of times gone by. There was Taurus. There was Gemini. Cassiopeia sat up there alongside Perseus.

And there, looming up over the horizon, was Orion, the hunter.

Chris felt his fur twitch as he studied the rising constellation. Orion had been vitally important to the ancient Egyptians. Theory had it that they had even aligned the pyramids to match that set of stars.

Not many people knew that the Bloodline of Abel had been at its height during their culture too.

One thing Hawkins had taught him had been that the Bloodline had ruled Egypt with an iron fist, dictating laws and religions that kept the populace under their dominion for hundreds of years.

That had been the time of the Potency.

The stars above twinkled in Dootson's pupils as he remembered his creator waxing lyrical about this legendary stone. Cast from before time itself, it gave the Bloodline immense powers. It resonated with the harnessed power of the great abyss that flowed between the three states of Creation: the physical realm, the heavenly realm and Beyond.

The stargazer sighed.

That was all he knew. Hawkins had ended up as an ant supper before he could tell him anymore. Not that a newbie werewolf needed to know all about this mythical mumbo jumbo stuff. He would have been happy to just use his new enhanced eyesight to gaze at his beloved stars in the still darkness of night.

He may have the potential to be a skilful hunter like the mythological Orion, but truthfully that just wasn't for him. Once a month he came out here as far away from humans as possible, watched the stars and picked off the odd geriatric sheep or rabbit.

Speaking of which…

His stomach gave an impatient rumble and he rose to his feet, giving his shaggy, unkempt fur a brisk shake. Lifting his nose to the air, he inhaled deeply to locate his supper then frowned as something else caught his senses.

There was the crack of a gunshot and his shoulder burst open in agony.

The lycanthrope yelped as he tumbled over onto

4

his back. Quickly, he righted himself but kept low to the ground. What the hell was this? He glanced at his shoulder and observed blood oozing from a straight wound. Nowhere near fatal, but it stung like fury.

No one should be out here. It was always deserted when he came out for his monthly transformation. He made sure of that.

Then a thought crossed his mind. Perhaps the local farmer had gotten pissed off at his sheep being a noc-turnal supper once a month? He nodded slowly. That had to be it. The local Farmer Giles had decided to have a pot shot at what he must have thought was a fox or a stray dog.

Okay, all he had to do was keep low and quiet. He could crawl away without being seen. Right now the farmer probably just thought he was a large German shepherd or some such. If he got away, there would be no need to take more drastic action. The last thing he wanted was pictures plastered all over the *Lancaster Chronicle* of The Beast of Bowland.

The question was, in which direction was the idiot with the gun?

The answer came to this as another shot flattened him onto his front.

This time Chris saw red and the offspring of Abel sprang up onto his hind legs snarling viciously in the dir-ection of the shooter. He felt his blood pump around his body, not his mortal, human blood, but that which had been born from the bite of his creator. It coursed through his veins and surged out to the capillaries of his gunshot wounds. Dootson stood tall and fearless as he felt the mere scratches begin to knit themselves together.

"Show yourself!" his guttural voice snarled into the

dark.

A dark which was suddenly brighter than the stars above.

Chris reflexively shielded his eyes as harsh arc lights flared into life all around him, encircling him in a prison of light. The sound of a boot on the grass made him attempt to turn around, but the blazing agony of a cattle prod to his back caused him to fall to the ground once more.

The wolf rolled and lunged at its attacker.

Another burst of electricity stunned him from a different direction.

Then another.

Then another.

Dootson vainly tried to lash out at his unseen assailants but they were skilfully fast and the lights were too bright. Again and again the cattle prods brought him to his knees until finally he could not bring himself to retaliate any more.

"Enough," came a voice from behind the lights.

The electric shocks stopped and Chris was aware of the attackers withdrawing. He sat slumped in the muddy field, his eyes closed and his breathing erratic. What the hell was going on?

"Curious," it was the same voice – calm, superior, "I expected you to be somewhat larger in stature."

Chris wanted to snap back some sort of witty comment, but his throat was dry and his head ached. Instead, he just slowly opened his eyes and looked up at the man who stood before him, then frowned.

This was just getting weirder and weirder.

For a moment, he thought that the guy was Vladimir Putin. He was stood in front of a row of black clad goons armed with cattle prods and he wore just combat trousers and boots. He held a hunting rifle in his arms and a leather pouch was hanging from his neck. The weary wolf shook his aching head and took another look at his tormentor. No, it wasn't the Russian President come to hunt new prey in the wilds of Lancashire. This guy was taller, possessed fancier hair and was decidedly ripped. There was more definition to his abs than there was in the latest wide screen television.

Chris cocked his head to one side and frowned in curiosity as he felt the effects of the cattle prods begin to subside.

"So," continued the not-Putin, "I guess you're wondering why I am here right now. Well," he continued, not letting Chris answer, "I am here to claim something that I feel is rightfully mine.

"I have been watching your kind for many years now, inserting themselves in positions of power and influence. It's quite skilful how you've accomplished what you have without drawing attention to yourselves. I'm impressed, truly.

"But I think it's time for a change.

"Time for new management."

Chris laughed, his dry chuckle distorted by his lupine form.

"You find this funny?"

"You've got the wrong guy. You think I can give you power? I'm nobody! I just fix people's TV aerials."

The stranger smiled and Chris' laugh evaporated in the cold air around him. "You've got it wrong," the bare-chested man said, handing his rifle to one of his lackeys. "You're not going to *give* me your power; I'm going to *take it*." Then he threw himself at the unsuspecting werewolf.

Well, tonight is just going from bad to worse, Chris thought to himself as the half-naked crazy guy flew through the air at him. The aerial fitter-cum-werewolf tried to bat his assailant away, but the attacker was apparently quite skilled as he turned at the last minute and dived in behind the lycanthrope's arm.

Chris reached around and tried to grab at the man's head but damn he was quick! A sharp elbow jabbed down into his shoulder and he felt his legs buckle underneath the combined weight of himself and his attacker.

What was this guy? Some sort of ninja?

As he fell to the floor for what felt like the hundredth time that night, Chris rolled and slammed his back into the front of the maniac. Most people would have yelled out or gone limp, stunned. Not this guy. He shouted out in glee and went with the blow, levering with his legs and rolling Chris onto his front.

The werewolf arched his spine and heaved himself backwards, desperate to dislodge his foe, but the man was firmly clamped onto him and he felt blow after blow rain down onto his shoulders and his head.

This was no joke.

This guy was too good!

Mustering all the energy he could, Chris tensed himself before springing forward in a thrusting leap. He was aware of the bright lights drawing rapidly closer before they were directly above him. He spun and careened into the pole that was holding a lamp up. There was a satisfying grunt as the guy on his back was smacked directly between a wolf and a hard place.

Chris felt the grip on his pelt loosen and he pulled

8

away, shaking his head to regain his composure.

However, this did not stop the attacker. He flew at his quarry once more, but this time Chris was ready and did likewise. They met mid-air in a barrage of teeth, fists and claws. The man was relentless, pounding fist after fist into Chris' rapidly bruising body. The wolf retaliated by feinting with his snapping jaws and batting with the backs of his powerful claws.

He knew he was at somewhat of a disadvantage. He could despatch this guy with one lucky blow. He could swipe across his throat and rip the breath from his lungs, or he could latch on with his vicious teeth and rip him to shreds.

Or he could do worse.

He could just bite him. The human would be defeated and the wolf inside would rise.

But he didn't want to do any of these. He just wanted to be left in peace. So, instead, he just parried blow after blow and looked for a way to immobilise his enemy without any permanent damage.

All the while, the voice in the back of his head screamed for him to submit, to go full out and rip his powerful opponent to shreds.

It was so hard to resist.

With every attacking punch, every deflected blow, the centuries' old voice within him cried out for more. It wanted blood. It craved its taste.

With each attack assailed upon his body, the blood inside of Chris cried out for revenge.

And his attacker knew it.

"Yes. There it is," he grinned as he smacked another well-placed fist into the wolf's face. "I can see it in your eyes. It wants to hurt me, doesn't it? It wants to destroy me."

Chris flinched as he blocked another right jab.

"Why don't you feed its hunger? Why don't you give it what it wants? You are of the Bloodline. You were born from vengeance. Come on! Release that anger!"

The man spun round and kicked Chris in the head. The battered wolf howled in pain. This was too much.

He just wanted to be left in peace.

He just wanted to watch the silent stars.

He just wanted to…

Another kick darted through the air.

He just wanted to…

Chris caught it firmly between the claws of his left hand.

He just wanted to… kill…

Twisting hard, the descendant of the wronged child of Adam, dragged his unknown attacker down into the cold mud. Snarling frantically, the wolf pounced and was suddenly upon the bare chest of the mere mortal. The savage beast pulled its lips back and cruel teeth glistened in its widening mouth.

Enough! This was enough!

It plunged its mouth down for the final bite…

…and stopped.

The man was not retaliating. He was lying there, his neck open, undefended, waiting for the bite.

The wolf lowered its face to that of this curious foe and studied it. Slowly, it sniffed at its beaten prey, taking in the combined smell of dirt, sweat, adrenaline and expensive aftershave. Its eyes scrutinised the perfect face that looked defiantly up from its prone, defeated position.

Defeated.

Was it really?

"Who are you?" asked the wolf.

"I am the future," replied the man. "Now do what you rightly should."

The man who repaired aerials and studied stars looked through the eyes of the wolf at the lunatic beneath him before slowly backing off. "No," he growled. "I don't know who you are, or what's going on in that bitch crazy head of yours, but you do not want… this."

The man dragged himself to his feet and pawed distractedly at the leather pouch that hung from his neck. "Oh, but I do. Trust me I do. Hold him," he nodded towards the confused wolf.

Chris was aware of a number of arms latching onto him. He flexed his muscles and started to wrestle free when bizarrely, all his strength evaporated and he sank to his knees. "What the hell?" he managed to squeak out of his tight throat.

The man stood in front of him, his leather pouch open and a green hemispherical stone clasped firmly in his right hand. An ethereal mist seeped out from its polished surface. The tendrils reached out and caressed Dootson's fur. Lazily, knowing they could not be harmed, they eased their way into his ears and up inside his nostrils. Wanting to pull away, but unable to even blink, the werewolf was aware of everything around him fading into a green mist that washed across his blurred vision.

It was warm…

He was no longer knelt in a cold, muddy field in Lancashire. Hot sand scalded his knees and bright sunshine scorched his eyes.

Sunshine…

Chris looked down at his hands.

His paws.

He gasped as he stared up again into the bright blue sky. No moon hung above, surrounded by his beloved starscape. No Orion hunted in the dark.

He was aware of movement all around him. Other wolves stepped out confidently into the light of day.

In front of them, dominating the square in which they congregated, stood an imposing statue of a man with the head of a wolf. In its outstretched hand was a gleaming green gemstone.

All around, howling reached through time…

The green haze dissipated and Chris was left staring up into the manic grin of his captor.

"What was that?" His voice felt as distant as the Andromeda galaxy. "The past?"

"The future," the bare-chested man smiled. His eyes flicked to one of the goons that held Dootson. "Take it."

Chris winced as he felt a needle slide into his arm. Weakly, he tried to pull away, but still he felt unable to move. He could only watch as his conqueror held out his arm to the needle. "No…" the beaten wolf moaned as he watched whilst his blood was injected into the victor. "Why?"

The man flung back his head and half shouted, half howled as the effect of the Bloodline began to take hold. Before Dootson's eyes he watched as man became wolf.

When the transformation had finished, the newest member of the Bloodline of Abel took his brother by the paw and lifted him to his feet. "Come," he said. "We have an empire to build."

Somebody's Gotta Do It

Yeah, well it's not the most prestigious of jobs, I know, but it has its perks. I'm always warm and snuggled up in here. The socks provide plenty of insulation and it's not as if they're minging or anything. They're always laundered before they're put away, so my home smells like lavender or jasmine or even just a nice, plain detergent. I like that. Sometimes the simple one's the best. I remember this time they tried a summer fruits fragrance. Dear lord, how I laughed. I smelt like a bleedin' satsuma for a month.

Yeah, it's a nice place to live.

And the socks taste great too.

Haha, yeah everyone looks at me like that when I say that. I guess most of you folk have never bitten into a sweet mixture of cotton, nylon and elastane and thought to yourself: *Now, that's the ticket.*

I don't eat much, just the occasional nibble now and then. Enough to fill me up, like. But I do enjoy it.

Mind you, I don't think them out there are too keen on the idea. I hear the drawer open, see the socks get tossed around like a fabric salsa verde and then hear all sorts of words that would make my dear departed Gran blush when they find yet another one bearing unexplained holes.

I mean, there's no need for *that*, is there? After all, we've all gotta live, haven't we? I'm sure they go out and eat things that inconvenience others. Think of those poor little lambs they're so keen on. I bet their mothers aren't so happy seeing them served up with mint sauce, but do you see them going on Jeremy Kyle, effing and blinding? It's the way of the world. But, no, when it happens to *them*...

There was this one time when they really lost their rag. They started dragging out all the socks, shouting and cursing as they did. I didn't understand a word, not speaking their lingo, but I certainly got the gist of it, if you know what I mean. It's hard not to when the volume goes up and all your world's being thrown around the room. Anyways, they yanked each and every sock out of the drawer, even the old single ones right at the back where I put my feet up after a hard night's munching. Yeah, there was no call for that. They left me with nothing. I had to hide right at the back of the drawer, scrunching myself down into the wood. That's 'cos I'm not allowed to be seen, you know. It's part of the job.

All day they left me like that: cold, exposed. I was right unhappy, I can tell you. I got so far as to having a peek out of the drawer. You won't tell anyone, will you? So, all I could see was pile upon pile of discarded socks up on their bed. I was sorely tempted to just nip out and grab a few, drag 'em back into my gaff and snuggle up to get warm. But then there would be questions wouldn't there? They'd ask each other who moved the damn things and, when it was apparent that neither of them had, they would investigate.

And we don't want that, do we?

It's not good for all parties concerned.

Trust me.

Like I said, they're not supposed to know about me. I live here, all quiet like, having my fill of their cotton footwear and just minding my own business. I leave them alone. They buy new socks or repair the old ones and life carries on all hunky dory.

It don't go to upset the status quo.

That's happened once before. It weren't nice.

So, yeah back to the story. Eventually they replaced the socks. I mean, who wouldn't? If you've got a sock drawer, then you need to fill it with socks. It stands to reason, doesn't it? So I was all warm and happy to chow down again.

But I reckon things aren't all that they used to be out there these days.

How do I know?

Well, I've been around the block a few times and I've learnt to read the signs. I learnt to look after myself over the years. There are those certain little warning signs that things aren't what they should be. The first is the quality of the socks. I don't mean the fabric, the material. Nah, it don't matter what you make 'em out of, they all taste fine to us. What does leave a metaphorical taste in my mouth though is when the thickness of the material changes. It can happen from time to time, normally when there's a new shop opened and one of them has decided to save a bit of cash for a few weeks. They come home pleased as punch with their new purchase, all smiles and whatnot, but it doesn't last. In a week or so, after the socks have been worn just a couple of times, they realised that they've been suckered in by that old monster: False Economy.

The thing is, you get what you pay for, don't you? Expensive socks are better made, thicker. They last longer. These shoddy cheap things... Well they end up with holes when I've not even had a nibble! Not that I would as they just don't fill me up. I'd have to take a far larger chunk out their hosiery than normal and that would *really* cause suspicion. They'd go beyond thinking it's moths and shoving those stinking ball things in the drawer. Jeez! The last time they did that I needed to get the fumigator in. It was worse than the times they get a pet puppy and it... well, you know what puppies are prone to do.

It was when the fumigator came that I learned about Fred.

What a sorry tale that was.

He'd had the same thing happen to him. Fred had been a nice, quiet guy. Kept himself to himself – perhaps a bit too much, if you know what I mean. He weren't one for nipping down the pub in an evening or having mates over to his drawer to tuck into the latest silk stockings. No, he was quite the loner.

If he'd had mates to talk to when those kids took him on, perhaps it would have turned out different, like?

The young 'uns are always a problem. Always turning things upside down and looking into things for no bloody reason. Well, Fred's humans had these two kids who were far brighter than they should have been. You see, when they kept getting the blame for putting holes in their best cotton socks, they decided that summat was afoot and they decided to investigate.

First, they tried the moth balls. Apparently our Fred

was none-to-happy about this, but he tolerated the inconvenience and got it sorted. But then the kids tried other things. First there was salt. Fred thought they were having a laugh, didn't he? He reckoned they must have thought he was a slug or summat.

It was when they realised the salt hadn't worked that things got nasty.

One morning, Fred woke up to the most godawful smell and, what was worse, he had blood running out of his nose. He tried to stand but found that his legs couldn't bear his weight. Something was dreadfully wrong. He noticed that there was another substance in his drawer, his home. It was a thin grey powder that drifted up into the air every time he moved.

There was only one thing that he could do.

Carefully, when he was sure that no one was around, he heaved himself up out of the drawer and on to the kids' bed. It was one of those big double metal affairs. Well, Fred leant against the ladder, breathing heavily as the clearer air started to do him the power of good and he looked around, having a good sniff, like.

We have a really good sense of smell. We need to in order to discern which socks are gonna be the freshest and tastiest. Although there are those amongst us who have, what shall we say, a *thing* for less than clean hosiery. But I won't go into those little peccadillos right now.

Back to Fred.

He stood on the bed and let his nose guide him. He climbed up onto a small chest of drawers and there, in front of him was a can that positively reeked of whatever it was that the kids had laced his home with.

I can't say for sure what it was that finally pushed Fred over the edge. I mean, we're simple folk, really. We keep ourselves to ourselves. Perhaps it was the relentless bullying, the invasion of his home? Perhaps it was just the indignity of having one pulled over him by a pair of snotty-nosed brats? Whatever it was, Fred stood looking at that tin and something inside him snapped, pushed him over the line.

He was only a little chap, but a determined one. I can't credit the amount of grit and effort it must have taken him to do what he did, but he got the desired results that's for sure, much to our horror. Apparently you could hear their mother's screams from outside the house when she found the kids the next day. He'd waited until they were sleeping soundly in their nice cosy beds then taken the can of stuff and poured it carefully down their snoring mouths. Next, to make sure it stayed there, he grabbed a load of socks and pushed them down their throats to seal the deal. Don't ask me how he managed it. I wasn't there. Perhaps he tied the kids down? Perhaps they were just sound sleepers? Whatever the case, apparently the result was... horrible.

None of us know what happened to Fred. Some say he went and offed himself, unable to live with what he did. Some say he gave up on the sock business and went to live in a cave away from those who ruined his life.

Me? I say, "Once a sock monster, always a sock monster."

I reckon he's out there somewhere, tucked down nice and cosy in the back of some unsuspecting soul's sock drawer. Someone who is unaware that there's a killer in their bedroom.

Perhaps he's in yours?

Frank's Castle

"So, Mister Mulligan,"

"Oh, please call me Frank."

Giggles slightly. "Oh, okay. So, *Frank*, would you like to tell the listeners why on Earth you bought this castle?"

"Well, Judy, what can I say? I guess it's the age-old dream of many young lads to run around the ramparts of a mediaeval fortification and pretend they're Robin of Hood or the Sheriff of Nottingham. So, when I won the lottery..."

"That was last December, wasn't it?"

"Indeed it was. Christmas came early!"

They both laugh.

"So, yes, when I had that unexpected windfall, I thought to myself, well what do I want to do? And I decided that, truth be told, I wanted to live my childhood dream." Shrugs nonchalantly.

"So you bought Dibchester Castle."

"I bought Dibchester Castle."

"Perhaps you can tell the listeners what attracted you to this particular edifice? Was it the beautiful grounds? I believe they are one of the best maintained mediaeval gardens in the country."

Head waggles from side to side. "To tell the truth, Judy, I've never really been an outdoorsy sort of chap. Flora and fauna have never really rocked my boat. When I was a young lad, I was always being scolded by my old man that I ought to get out more and that hiding up in my room was unhealthy. I tried to explain to him that I was reading up on various historical this and thats that they used to get up to in antiquity, but he would never have it. He always thought I ought to be out playing footie or riding my bike. No dear, I'm more drawn to the *internal* features of the castle." Strokes his chin. "Tell you what, why don't I show you?"

"Well I think the listeners would love that."

"Capital. Why don't you come this way then?" Leads Judy inside.

"So this is the courtyard?"

"Indeed it is. Apparently they held all manner of tournaments here. There was jousting, armed combat. Anything to catch the attention of the fair damsels." He winks. They both chuckle. "I suppose it was all very grand, but no, I'm far more interested in what lies over here."

"Shall we take a peek?"

"I think we shall. Now, you'll have to mind your step here slightly, Judy, as this part of the castle's never been open to the public, so it's a touch more *au naturel,* shall we say?"

Peers into the gloom. "I must say, it's rather dark, Frank."

"That's okay. Here we go. That better?"

"Oh yes. Is that an actual mediaeval torch?"

"It is indeed. It's sat here for about a thousand years. Can you imagine that? What sort of things has it seen?"

"That's truly amazing."

Nods in agreement. "Shall we go down?"

Giggles, albeit slightly nervously. "Oh, is there a dungeon down here?"

Winks mischievously. "We'll have to wait and see, won't we? After you, and do mind your step. Now, as you can see, this stone staircase goes down a *devil* of a long way. In fact, it's a testament to the building's architects that they managed to keep the whole thing up with this squirrelling away underneath."

"My, it's really starting to get quite chilly down here."

"Oh, not to worry, there's something at the end that'll warm you up. Just you wait and see. Yes, it's a very little-known part of the castle this, but as soon as I found it, I knew it would be right for me. Ah, here we are."

"My word, that's an incredibly hefty door, isn't it? How did they get it down here?"

"Oh, ropes and pulleys, I guess. Ropes and pulleys. They were for ever tying things up back then."

"Pardon?"

"Do mind the step." Guides her in. "There you go."

"Oh!" Startled. "The floor's wet! Does it get damp?" The door slams shut.

"Frank? Mister Mulligan! What are you doing?"

She feels liquid rain down on her in the dark.

"Mister Mulligan!" Screaming now in panic.

"Sorry, dear, I can't talk too much right now." Sounds breathy. "This old… crank... really is quite hard but it does spray the oil in quite a satisfactory manner."

"Oil?" Voice has risen an octave.

"Yes, dear. Oil. Ah, there we go. All done."

"Please… what are you doing?" Sees bright light tumbling down towards her.

"There we go." Feels content as the heat and screams rise up to meet him. "Just how I dreamt it would be. Lovely." Turns and carefully walks up the dark staircase to the bright light of day.

Not-So-Lucky Larson

"What if yesterday you were someone completely different?" – Sam Spallucci: Ghosts From The Past.

"One hundred and eighty!"

The Penny Bank erupted in a mighty explosion of cheers as Nick Larson swaggered up to the dart board and retrieved his darts. Returning to his pint, he gave a smug wink to his opponent who just shook his head and stood up on the oche. Larson couldn't miss the perspiration on his rival's brow. The fifty quid sat in the glass on the table would be his in three shots, he was sure of it.

"You've got the bugger on the ropes."

"He's two twenty against my three sixty. Guess you'll be wanting a double in five minutes?" Larson grinned at his drinking partner over the top of his pint glass.

One dart hit the board. Fifteen.

"Just one?" Mick asked. "You being tight?"

The second dart hit. Three.

"Hey, this is my hard-earned cash, not your liquor money."

23

The third dark hit metal and pinged off wildly to the side.

The crowd groaned.

The disheartened player cursed loudly.

Larson downed the rest of his drink, belched and approached the oche. He checked his watch. Quarter past nine. Okay, that meant he could finish this off with three shots, grab another round and safely be home for ten. Work tomorrow. Wouldn't do to be hung over. He didn't even bother with a smirk at the deflated opponent, instead he threw the darts at the board in rapid succession.

Treble twenty.

Treble nineteen.

Double twelve.

The pub erupted in a discordant cheer as the victor first collected his darts, then his winnings.

"You lucky bugger," Mick laughed as Larson handed him his drink. "I'll never know how you manage that."

Nick raised his glass at his drinking partner and saluted him: "Anything is possible!"

It was only a little bit after ten and a couple of rounds later as the two mates walked with a gentle swaying motion up Bowerham Road. "Seriously though," the words crawled drunkenly out of Mick's mouth for the fifth time, "I really don't know how you do it. You are just *so* damned lucky."

Larson sighed. "It's all mindset, like I said before. If you expect to lose, then you will. Likewise, if you expect to win, then that will be the outcome, and a more desirable one at that."

Mick shook his head in such a manner that the

whole world swayed somewhat. "I dunno. Sounds like all those crappy self-motivational memes you get on Facebook."

They drew to a stop outside a nicely-sized semi-detached house. "I've told you before, it's nothing like that."

His mate grunted. "Sounds all very dodgy to me. I mean, come on, loads of you at the Ashton Hall on a Wednesday, listening to some guy… Bit creepy."

Nick closed his eyes. *Here we go again*: he thought. "He's not like that. Malcolm's a genuine bloke. You ought to see the things he can do." He frowned as his friend expelled a derisive sound. "Okay, so what about me? I was a mess before he came along. You never knew the *old* me, back then. Let me reassure you, I was a complete waste of space. Yet now my life is just… perfect. Great job, great house, great wife. You can't argue with that, can you?"

Mick gave a non-committal shrug. "Perhaps," he surrendered slightly. "Perhaps. Anyway, I'd better get going. See you Saturday, Lucky Larson?"

"Sure will," Nick smiled and watched his best mate sway off along the road.

He turned and walked up the path to his house. His house where his wife would be waiting, safe in the knowledge that he would be home only a little bit later and just a touch squiffier than promised.

But it hadn't always been like that.

Dear god, no it hadn't.

Six months ago he had been sleeping on the sofa, fully expecting each night to be his last under the roof of his marital home. It was safe to say that he had been a reckless kind of guy, the sort who just said, "To hell with it!" and would have to pick up the pieces at a later date if he could remember where he'd left the damned things. His work had suffered, meaning no fat bonuses. Bills hadn't been paid. Promises weren't kept. Trust was gradually eroded away.

Then one day, the day that he had fully expected to be shown the door by Wendy, Nick had decided that enough was enough. Rather than heading to work, he had walked in the opposite direction along Bowerham Road, right up and out of town until he had reached the busy M6 motorway. He had looked like total crap: unshaven, uncombed and crumpled. He had felt even worse. For the last month, insomnia had been his nighttime companion as unforgiving upholstery had repeatedly berated him for his failures, but the previous night had just been unbearable. For once, he had slept - but he had dreamt.

And what dreams they had been. Nightmares the like of which he had never endured before and never wanted to submit to ever again.

He had felt cold things slithering round him and wrapping him in constricting muscles. They had pulled him tight, blocking off his breath, yet he would not die. He lay there gasping for air for what seemed like hour after hour. As he did, he saw all the things in his life that were suffocating him: his pressured job, too many bills, a wife who shunned him.

So, when he woke, he realised that enough was enough.

This found him climbing down the steep embankment to the motorway on the edge of Lancaster. He stumbled down onto the hard shoulder and didn't even pause. He staggered onto the carriageway, faced the oncoming traffic, his eyes closed and his arms stretched out, awaiting the inevitable sweet release from his personal hell.

It came in a most unexpected way.

"I think you'd better come with me."

Nick Larson felt a firm but gentle grip on his arm lead him back onto the hard shoulder where a sleek, expensive-looking car was parked, its hazard lights flashing. He looked up into the most curious orange-coloured eyes and just croaked impotently as he tried to speak.

"No need," came the soft, enchanting voice. "Just let me help you."

"Morning sweetie."

Nick smiled, his eyes still shut as he felt his wife of fifteen years snuggle up close to him. "Morning beautiful. Sleep well?"

"Like a log. Coffee?"

"Mmmm… Yes please." His eyes followed the beautiful blonde woman out of the room as he swung his legs from beneath the rich bedclothes and started to dress himself. By the time he had showered, shaved and made himself presentable, the rich aromatic smell of Atkinson's Origin had permeated around the house.

"Don't forget to pick up something for Anthea, will you?"

Nick nodded. His sister-in-law was loveable but notoriously hard to buy for. "I've seen something in that little place down on King Street. You know, that new gallery?"

"Oh, fabulous! Sounds perfect."

Nick downed the coffee, grabbed a slice of toast and picked up his briefcase. "I'd better get going. I'll have to grab some cash on the way to work. I don't think they take plastic."

"Okay sweetie," Wendy kissed his buttery lips and giggled. "Have a good one."

"Of course I will. I always do."

"Well that's odd."

It was the third cash machine that Nick had visited on his way to work and the third one that had not recognised his PIN. He checked his watch: ten to nine. He couldn't visit his bank yet and he had to get to work, so he decided to nip out at lunchtime and withdraw some cash over the counter. Perhaps his card had got scratched? He checked the chip before he slipped it into his wallet. It looked fine. Very odd. He pulled open the rear door to Boots and cut through the shop on the way to his office. It was going to be a busy one. He had three deals to wind up so had to make sure that he was up to date with his notes. One by one he ticked off various tasks he had to knock on the head in order to make sure things ran smoothly, niftily dodging the early morning shoppers as he did so.

He reached the automatic doors at the front of the shop.

They refused to open.

Larson looked up at the motion sensor and walked up to the doors again.

Nothing.

He shook his head and left via the manual door to the left before continuing his morning walk to his office on Market Street.

By lunchtime, two of the contracts had been assured and the appropriate papers had been emailed out

to relevant parties, ready to be printed, signed and returned. He would have cleared number three, leading to
a nice quiet afternoon, but the client in question, one Mr
Graham Henderson of Tunstall and Sons Factoring, had
skipped out for an early lunch. The polite secretary on the
other end of the line promised to inform Mr Henderson
that Nick had rung and that her boss would be eagerly
awaiting his call that afternoon.

Nick smiled. Ah well, two out of three wasn't bad.
He *would* seal the third deal that afternoon. He *knew* he
would, so it would definitely happen.

Anything was possible.

Yes, anything was *truly* possible. Over the last few
months he had been witness to some incredible things:
drunks had become sober; junkies had cleaned themselves up; toxic relationships had been healed.

But that had not been the end of it.

As Larson stepped out onto Market Street and
headed for his bank, he recalled the truly miraculous.
Those who had been paralysed had once more been able
to walk; the eyesight of the blind had been returned to
them; those who could not talk had been handed back
their voices.

All at the hands of one man.

Malcolm Wallace.

He truly was amazing. He showed that indeed anything was possible. A mantra to live your life by.

So Nick Larson did and, as a result, he had started
to turn heads. He nailed those lucrative contracts; he got
the best seats in the nicest restaurants; he even had a
killer darts game. That was why he was known by so
many as *Lucky* Larson.

Luck.

Nick smiled. Luck had nothing to do with it. It was all positive attitude. Pay attention to the little things in life and larger things fall into place. Be polite to those who others ignore and make them feel valued and they then go on to run that extra mile for you. Put in that extra bit of prep and impress those with power and wealth so they will be happy to share with you that which is theirs.

So it was that Nick smiled politely at the young cashier in the bank as he explained that he was having problems with his card and asked to take some money out over the counter. The young lad said nothing, swiped the card and just grunted, "Can't."

"Pardon?"

"Account doesn't exist," the youth shrugged. "You must have closed it."

Larson frowned. "No, I assure you that I haven't. I used it just yesterday evening."

"No, you didn't."

"Erm, yes I did."

"Doesn't exist. Can't have done."

For a moment, no words came from Larson's stunned mouth. Then he took a breath, composed himself, smiled and asked, "Why don't I speak to someone who can sort this?"

"On lunch. Come back later." With that, the verbally challenged boy drew down his blind. Conversation over.

Too stunned to pursue the matter further, the perturbed Larson left the bank and headed back to his office.

What the hell was going on?

Back at his desk, he decided that Plan B was in order. No cash meant no visit to the gallery. He would have a quick browse online. Calling up a site he had used regularly, he found a rather nice piece of brightly glazed pottery. Thinking about how much Anthea would love it, he chose next day delivery and logged in. After checking the total, he clicked on the pay button, using his already stored card details.

A red error flashed up: *card not recognised*.

What the hell?

He tried again.

And again.

He checked the details against his Visa. They matched. This was crazy. He entered the details of his debit card, meticulously reading each number three times and tried with that.

Card not recognised.

Larson's heart sank as realisation started to dawn. His account had been hacked. It had to have been. That explained everything. He would have to ring the bank and get them to put a stop on his account.

Just then an alarm rang on his mobile. He checked it and swore quietly. The bank would have to wait; he had to ring Mr Henderson back.

The phone rang three times in his ear and was picked up by the same secretary as before.

"Hi, Nick Larson here."

"Sorry? Who?"

"Nick Larson. We spoke this morning. I said that I would ring Mr Henderson after lunch."

There was a pause. "I'm sorry but Mr Henderson is not expecting any phone calls this afternoon."

Nick nervously ran his fingers through his hair. "But we spoke just this morning."

"I can assure you, sir, that we did not."

He frowned. He had been sure that it had been the same receptionist. "Okay, well would it be possible to talk to Mr Henderson? It's about the Luneside development."

"What exactly about the Luneside development?"

"I was brokering the deal between him and Mr Stone."

There was another pause. "I'm sorry, sir, but that account has already been agreed."

Nick just stared at the phone. *What the hell?*

He was aware of a faint voice saying something else but it clicked off as he replaced the handset in its cradle.

This wasn't happening. How? Just how was this possible? He *had* spoken to Henderson's receptionist this morning. Hell, he had been working for months on this deal! Larson turned to his computer and clicked to the Henderson folder.

At least, he tried to.

It wasn't there.

No. This isn't happening...

He needed a drink.

"Well that sucks."

Nick Larson sighed disconsolately over his comforting pint. Mick had joined him after receiving a rambling message about the day from hell. "Tell me about it! I mean, what's happening, man?"

"Dunno. You want another?"

Nick nodded. "You paying?" He had spent the remains of last night's winnings on the previous two rounds.

"Sure. Same again?"

Nick nodded once more. "I'm going for a slash." He heaved himself up and headed to the toilets. After relieving himself of three pints of beer, he turned, washed his hands and then held them under the automatic dryer.

Nothing happened.

"Come on," he grumbled, waving them around from side to side. Nothing. Not a breath of hot air. "Bloody typical." He wiped his hands on his suit trousers and headed back into the bar just as his mobile began to ring.

It was Wendy.

"Hey."

"Hi sweetie. You okay?"

"Sure. Just a rough day."

"Oh right, it's just, well it's almost seven."

Seven?

"Oh God, I'm sorry. Really sorry. It was the day from hell at work and I went to the Penny Bank."

"Oh."

Shit!

"Listen, I'm really sorry. I'll drink up and head home. Okay?"

"Okay."

"Love you."

"Love you too. See you in a bit." She hung up.

Nick cursed under his breath as he made his way back to his table where a fresh pint was waiting.

"S'up?"

"I'm in trouble at home now."

"The day gets better and better then?"

"Tell me about it."

He downed his in three long draughts. "Listen, I gotta go."

"Sure. Listen. It'll all be something or nothing."

Nick nodded and headed off home.

"This cannot be happening…"

Okay, he had consumed a few beers, but he wasn't

that drunk. However, try as he may, he could not get his obstinate key to fit into the lock of his front door.

"Stupid, bloody…"

Nick took a step back, careful not to stumble into his pristine flowerbed. He looked at the number on the door. Yep. That was the right one. He twisted around and surveyed the street. That was correct too. He pulled the key up close to his eyes. It certainly *looked* right.

He tried again.

It was nowhere near a match.

Jesus, the day gets better and better…

Leaning his aching head on the hard door, he rapped loudly with his knuckles. A few seconds later, the door opened. "Yes?"

"Wendy, something's up with my key."

There was silence.

"Wendy?"

"I… Who are you?"

Nick braced himself against the doorframe as the world swayed violently and he concentrated on looking at the slippered feet that stood on the threshold to stop himself from keeling over.

"Come on Wendy, please let me in."

"I don't know you," came the female voice.

The drunk sighed. "I'm sorry. I should have rung, I know. I just forgot. It's been a horrid day. I'm sorry. Please just let me in." He wobbled as he looked up at the eyes peering out at him.

They didn't belong to his wife.

"Where's Wendy?"

"Who?"

"Wendy. My wife." Larson tried to look behind the stranger and called into the house, "Wendy! It's Nick! I'm sorry."

The woman placed a hand on his chest and pushed him backwards. "There's no one here by that name. Now, please go before I call the police." She slammed the door in his face.

This was not happening.

This was *seriously* not happening.

Lawson carefully stepped back from the door of the building that should be his house, turned and walked out onto Bowerham Road, the street where he had lived with his wife for so many years.

Just one word went through his head: *What..?*

He pulled his phone out of his pocket and dialled Mick.

There was nothing, just three beeps then silence.

He tried again. Again there were three beeps then silence.

Running his fingers through his hair, he headed up the road to his friend's house.

For the second time that night, Nick Lawson found himself knocking hopelessly on a front door. It swung inwards and Mick was stood there. "Hello?"

"Some weird shit's happening at my house."

Silence.

"Can I crash here?"

"Who the hell are you?"

"Mick? Seriously? It's me. Nick."

His friend leant forward. "Listen buddy, I think you've had one too many, so I'll give you a break, but if you're not out of here in five seconds, I'll be throwing you off my property, okay."

Nick just stood and stared as his reality continued to implode.

"Seriously, mate. Get lost."
So he did.

The traffic roared in his ears as Nick Larson clambered down the all-too-familiar embankment. He slipped as his feet gave way and felt his once pristine suit rip, his shins barking on the rough surface.

He didn't mind the pain, though. The pain was real. Unlike him.

What had happened? Where had it all gone wrong?

He had followed the mantra. Anything is possible. And it had been. Success had been his as he had dragged his life out of the gutter.

And now he was right back where he had started six months ago.

A car horn blatted at him as he swayed unsteadily on his feet, the rush of air pushing him to one side like a toddler playing with its food.

Anything is possible: he thought to himself. All he had to do was believe in himself and he could correct this terrible mistake. He had been saved before; he would be saved again.

Traffic whipped by as he put first one foot, then another onto the carriageway. Cars swerved and horns screamed out as they had done half a year ago. Larson closed his eyes and faced the oncoming traffic once again, his arms stretched out to his sides.

Malcolm Wallace had saved him.

Malcolm Wallace had come and rescued him once before; he would do so again.

But, unknown to poor Nick Larson, his once saviour had met a fateful end over fifteen years ago, ripping him from existence and changing the lives of all those who had been touched by his insidious, grasping reach.

Malcolm Wallace did not come.

An articulated truck, however, did.

Here There Be Dragons

"When dragons walk the Earth, then all creation shall tremble." – Sam Spallucci: Ghosts From The Past.

Click.

He sighed and looked up at the clock. How long had it been now? He seemed to have been waiting for ever.

For *eternity.*

The man shifted his somewhat hefty rear against the hard unforgiving contours of the cheap plastic waiting room chair. Why couldn't they just fork out for something a bit more comfortable? Had the NHS come to this – removal of even the slightest trace of comfort? Even the tiniest nod to the god of padded materials would have been appreciated. Mind you, perhaps it was a cleanliness thing? If a patient had what was politely described as an *accident,* then it would probably be an excruciating job to clean up the mess if it had soaked into all-embracing velour. Hell, it would most likely stain and that would just make the waiting room appear skanky.

Not that it was the Hilton right now.

Click.

Just how old was that clock? A brown plastic shell, with large digital figures that tripped over every minute, it was a relic from a bygone era.

Somewhat akin to how the man saw himself. That was why he didn't go out much these days. Everything was just so... He fought for the correct word. *Different.*

It just wasn't like it had been in the past. Before...

Before what?

He closed his eyes and let his head lean back against the less than stable partition.

There was something. Something he should remember. It was important.

A church?

He shook his head and opened his eyes.

Click.

Why the hell was he thinking about a church? Had he ever set foot inside of one? He couldn't remember. Surely he must have as a kid? Back in his carefree days of youth. His parents would have dressed him up in his best clothes and dragged him off to the weekly ritual which was more social than spiritual, where he would spend his time barking coughs of protest at the insidious incense and longing for the biscuits that came afterwards, accompanied by weak orange squash.

But he remembered none of this.

No church. No biscuits.

No childhood. No parents.

What the hell had happened?

Click.

He hated clocks. All around him were timepieces counting down the hours, minutes, seconds of a life wasted. What did he do with his days? He sat around his house watching daytime television, stuffed deep into a threadbare sofa, as couples quarrelled about mundane rubbish, stuff that was of no consequence.

They shouted abuse at each other.

"You are mistaken!"

The man frowned. No, they didn't say that, did they? They shouted things which were far crasser and hurtful before big men in suits came on and dragged them off to calm down. All for public entertainment, of course.

"You are mistaken!"

And yet those three words rang out and cut him far deeper. Why? Who had said them? His mysteriously vanishing parents? He frowned as the face of a younger man coalesced in his head. Definitely not his hypothetical progenitors.

Click.

These memory gaps were driving him to distraction.

And then there were the dreams, which had brought him to this waiting room.

"Why don't you tell me about them?"

"The dreams?"

The doctor nodded silently, his mouth smiling benignly behind his neatly trimmed, *I'm an approachable professional* beard.

The man lay back on the couch. At least this was more comfortable than the infernal chair in the waiting room. He shifted his bulk into the soft padding. "There are so many," he said. "I don't know where to begin."

"Is there one that disturbs you more than the others? Perhaps one that stands out the most?"

The patient's eyes blinked shut. His internal screen

40

flickered into life, just like it did so many times at night, or even during his frequent daytime naps between so-called *reality* television shows. It was like the beginning of a main feature in a cinema, just like the ones you went to see as a kid with your parents, not that he had ever gone on such an outing nor possessed parents to take him, apparently.

There was blackness, and from the depths came sounds, distant at first, but gradually increasing in both volume and intensity. They were sounds of fighting: clashes of weapons, battle cries, screams of the doomed and dying. And above all of these were utterances the like of which no one had ever heard before. This was because the creatures from which they came could never have even existed. Screeches and roars caused the smallest of bones in his body to stutter and whine, made his spir-alled cochleae tremble. He was overcome with a violent nausea that caused him to perspire nervously as powerful odours assaulted his nose. Blood, sweat, fear and fire.

Then there was the unmistakable smell of scorched flesh: acrid yet sweet, charred yet aromatic. The man involuntarily licked his lips as the sources of this carnage came into view.

Atop a blasted battlefield, oblivious to all around them, two dragons fought each other with merciless in-tent: one red with seven heads, one the darkest obsidian. They screamed and slashed, inflicting gaping wounds in the scaled flesh of each other and, where their shredded skin fell, the ground beneath burst into flame. Trees were turned to ash, mountains to sand, earth to charcoal.

The patient opened his eyes. His cheeks were damp and his throat hoarse as he described the dreadful scene.

"Quite apocalyptic," the doctor mused.

The man silently nodded.

The was no sound except for the dry scratching of the doctor's pencil on a small notepad.

No sound in the room, that was. In the man's head, tortured screams still echoed until the doctor finally asked, "What of the other dreams? Are they all as traumatic?"

The man sighed. *Define traumatic*: he thought.

"There's a girl," he whispered.

The doctor sat, waiting for more.

"She's very pretty. Not a glamorous, made up artificial beauty. Not like those slags you see on telly. She's very natural. It's like she shines from inside. Her hair is unusual."

"In what way?"

"Well, sometimes it is pure blonde, like sun-baked sand. Yet other times there are red streaks in it."

"She dyes it?"

He shook his head against the couch as he stared up into this, the more pleasant of his memories. "No. It's natural. How can that be?"

The doctor gave no answer, instead he asked, "What are your feelings towards this girl?"

"I love her, unconditionally."

"Does she love you?"

"I… don't know. Sometimes, I think she does. Others…"

The doctor leaned forward. "Go on."

"I see terror in her eyes. Disgust too." He heard a slight sound from the doctor and turned to see the bearded man frowning. "What is it?"

"I have to ask… How *old* is this girl?"

"I don't know. It's all so vague. But I think she is younger than me. *Considerably* younger."

"Is she a child?"

"No! Dear god no. Actually, it feels more that *I'm* considerably older than *her*, if you know what I mean."

The doctor nodded and relaxed back into his chair. "I think so. Are there other dreams?"

Are there other dreams? The man exhaled a short breath. There were so many. Where to begin? Every night it was like he was watching a scene from a fantastical movie that was edited in a bizarre avant-garde fashion, chopping and changing plot and scene order, making no sense whatsoever.

There were ancient streets where sand crunched under his feet. There was a teenage boy with dark wavy hair and intense blue eyes. There was a cruelly smiling, raven-haired beauty who revelled in absolute adoration from the masses yet could only glance at him with vaguely hidden fear. Angels walked serenely around vast white halls and creatures of clay rose from the ground to destroy all who opposed their master.

Their master.

The man's stomach lurched as he heard indescribable sounds from a place he could not possibly begin to comprehend. A place where he stood encompassed by all that had been and would be. A place where he saw the wonders of humanity rise and fall before one man came and claimed reality as his own.

"*Kanor...*" he gasped.

The temperature dropped rapidly in the doctor's room. "What do you mean?"

"There is this man..."

The doctor leant forward with even more intensity

than before. "Tell me," he commanded.

"I see this man. He will perform unspeakable deeds. The world will be decimated, reduced to a faint shadow under his grasp. He longs for something he should not have. Some *things* he should never possess.

"A cup and a blade."

In the room, the man could hear the breathing of the medic increase in rapidity. In his mind, he saw the hooded man reach out with his scarred arm and declare, "*We are one!*"

"Tell me more about this person. Tell me about these things that he *desires*."

At first, the man thought that he had imagined the stress on the word, that his tension was playing tricks with his hearing. However, when he rolled his head on the couch to face the doctor, there was no mistaking what he saw.

Hunger.

The doctor's eyes betrayed a desperate feeling of longing, of want. Of *desire*.

The patient pulled himself up as he had the sudden urge to be as far away from here as possible.

"I need to go." He leapt from the couch, grabbed his things and quickly fled from the surgery.

It took him quite a while to realise that he was dreaming again. It was as if the desolate landscape around him was normal. It just felt like home as he viewed the decaying trees and scorched, withered grass.

It was pleasing to him. Comforting.

Around him, creatures of clay shambled about as if unsure of what their purpose was. He gazed upon them and truly studied them. They stood tall and broad, all legs and arms with a trunk for a torso and a squat dome atop for a head. As they approached him, they stood expectantly. If he said nothing, they turned and walked away. Computers with no programming. Soldiers with no commands.

The man sighed. What was this? *Where* was this?

He looked down and saw a dark cloak covering his skin, shrouding him from the single pin prick of light that hung in the early evening sky.

This dream was different to the others. He wasn't sure how; he just knew. As he cast his eyes around this devastated…

…*divergent*…

…landscape, he felt like he was peering through a lens, as if he were watching the world second hand.

A noise came from the darkened building behind him. A singing so sweet that it would have brought tears to his eyes had the body that he inhabited not forsaken its emotions centuries ago. Instead, he drew his sober cloak around him and re-entered the derelict church.

The song drew him along the nave and up the chancel to the high sanctuary where *They* dwelt. The joyous noise rang delicately in his ears as he gazed upon the objects of his desire. There, on the high altar lay the most beautiful things to ever exist: The Cup and The Blade.

Slowly, reverentially, he approached the objects of his desire, reaching out longingly with his hands. For a moment, his fingertips paused, uncertain that they should touch items so holy, when he owned a heart as black as a starless night, but then his hunger drove his hands forwards and he grasped them in his grip. As his pale skin wrapped around the enigmatic artefacts, songs erupted in his ears. Songs that came from within, not without. They told of aeons past when the Eternals rested in the Heavenly Realm. They exulted at the time before the creation of angels, when the only noise was their song.

They lamented having been apart for so long and rejoiced at their reuniting. Yet still there was a hole in their words. Still they lacked something.

And that was why it had not worked.

That was why everything was still here.

Try as he may, he could not bring about the end.

"When the Eternals are reunited, then all Creation shall fall," the voice of the creature under the hood rasped as he carefully lay his treasures back on the ancient stone table.

"They do not belong here," stated a voice from behind; a voice he had heard many times, millennia ago. "*You* do not belong here."

The creature under the dark cowl chuckled to himself. "Are you going to take them?"

"You know I will."

"And how do you expect to do that?"

There were rapid footsteps as the intruder quickened his pace up the nave. The sound of the Eternals rose higher than it had ever done before and their keeper drew upon this power as he spun to face his attacker. He felt his would-be assassin draw upon the same primordial strength and together they raised their right hands and declared:

"*We are one!*"

There was a flash of fire and a deafening thump of air pressure as two immense elemental powers blasted one another in the tattered chancel. At first, the flow of air seemed to batter the consuming flame back but then the song of the Eternals rose up into the air so that all could hear their jubilant chorus for miles around:

"He is here! He is here! He is here! Is it time?"

The cowled figure sank to his knees and felt the power of his attacker double, treble, quadruple. Slowly, metre by metre the inferno advanced upon him, pushing his own elemental weapon back until it was there at his fingertips, the tendrils of hell itself scorching the skin of his right arm.

The face of his attacker was gleeful at its apparent triumph.

But the creature was not yet done for.

He would never surrender.

He had waited so long for these beautiful treasures and their promised oblivion, that he would *never* give in.

Pulling on the one thing that he had left in his dwindling arsenal, the pain from his burning flesh, he rolled the agony up into a tight ball and commanded it to rise from the deepest pit of his stomach, up past his blackened heart which had once loved someone so dear to him, along his burnt arm and out, rocketing through his gnarled fingers.

The effect was cataclysmic.

The fire not only retreated but slammed his attacker back out the chancel, down the aisle towards the font that stood at the west end of the church, where he abruptly vanished.

The dreamer awoke.

Confusion perspired out of every pore as he gasped for air. Then, before he could examine his arm that seemed to burn like fury, the frigid air of the wintry morning assaulted his lungs and he fell to the floor, gasping and coughing in the frosty darkness.

Scrabbling around him for a clue as to what was happening, his eyes finally locked onto something that his frantic brain recognised as familiar, a rusty barbecue sat abandoned on the edge of a dirty patio in a neglected garden.

His garden.

How had he gotten here? Had he sleep walked?

He shakily ran his hand over his stubbled cheek then winced in shock. His fingers had scalded his skin and singed his scruffy facial hair. Lifting his right hand up before his eyes, confusion furrowed his brow. In his dream, pressurised air had blasted from his hand yet here, in the dimness of reality, tiny flames danced across chipped and bitten fingernails.

He blinked and they were gone.

He was just an overweight, middle-aged man stood in an overgrown garden early one December morning, staring at a perfectly normal hand. There were no flames. His arm was not charred, not mutilated by the fire of a night time attacker.

He needed a drink. Something cold.

Hurrying inside, he poured a glass of water and downed it as something tugged at him. His eyes were drawn to the old portable television on the grime-encrusted counter. For no reason that he truly understood, he flicked it on expectantly.

It was the national breakfast news. He was at once aware of the name of his town being mentioned and he frowned as images of the doctor's surgery were flashed up for all the country to see, to gawp at.

"Details are sketchy at the moment," reported a solemn man in a suit, "but the attack has experts completely baffled."

The man slumped down as he felt all strength start to seep out of his legs.

"Doctor Hudd was working late last night when someone apparently attacked him. From the damage to his surgery, the fire that the attacker caused was of an immense heat." The man noted the flashing of lights from fire engines in the background. "What we have been told so far, and this has yet to be verified by official sources, is that the circumstances of Doctor Hudd's death are indeed very unusual. Rather than burning as one might expect in the resulting blaze, he seems to have been preserved, baked as if he were like some sort of clay figurine in a kiln. The fire officer in charge…"

The watcher flicked off the television with a remote control that was awkwardly held together by duct tape.

Why had he fled the surgery yesterday? He had felt something from the doctor, something *wrong*.

Baked as if he were like some sort of clay figurine…

Images of the creatures stalking the barren landscape of his dream haunted him. Creatures of clay awaiting commands from their master.

He looked down at his hand and the sound of fighting dragons filled his head once more.

TV Dinner

As overacting cockneys raged at each other on the glaringly bright widescreen, Toby gnawed away enthusiastically at what had proven to be a somewhat troublesome repast.

Unaccustomed to fending for himself, the little chap was however finding a certain satisfaction in peeling away the tight layers that wrapped his meal.

When he hit bone, he couldn't help but wag his stubby little tail with excitement.

Wicked Intentions

"Horrid little scrotes!"

Baldwin ran his fingers through his lank greasy hair as he glowered at the smashed window. The third time in a month. The third time! His eyes shot up to the useless CCTV camera he'd installed last week. It seemed to be just perched idly on top of his fence, whistling innocently to itself.

"Useless piece of crap," he muttered, his worn moccasin grinding a piece of green tinted glass into the cracked asphalt. "Another waste of money." Sighing deeply, he fished out his old battered mobile and dialled for the repairer.

"This seems to be becoming a habit, Mister Baldwin."

"The little sods 'ave it in for me, don't they?"

The technician fiddled with the winding mechanism inside the door. "I wouldn't know about that. I just fit the glass."

"You see that?" Baldwin jabbed an angry finger up at the camera that allegedly watched them. "Guy who

51

sold it me last week said I'd 'ave no more trouble. No more trouble? The little buggers just gave it the finger before they smashed my bloody window."

Flicking a switch on the fascia of the door, the technician watched as the shiny new window slid up and down with ease. "There we go, anyway. All sorted."

"For 'ow long though, ay? 'Ow long?"

The technician stood up, carefully shut the car door and paused. "Listen," he said quietly, his eyes flitting up and down the alley, "I shouldn't really suggest this, but… Well, it doesn't seem fair you having to call me out every few weeks, does it?"

"Damn right it isn't."

"Anyway," he dug around in his overall pocket and produced a small grey card which he handed over to Baldwin, "there's this chap, see, who might be able to help you out?"

Baldwin eyed the card with great suspicion. "What *sort* of chap?"

The technician gave an uneasy shrug. "A witch-doctor." Then, as Baldwin made to open his mouth: "He's all above board. Registered and everything. One of the first ones to do so when they became legal last year. You might want to give him a bell." He motioned his head towards the new window. "Could save you a bob or two."

Baldwin flicked the glossy piece of card over and over between his fingers as his roll up slowly burnt its way towards his chapped lips. On the cracked monitor in front of him, a fuzzy image of three young hoodlums were frozen in a veil of static, each presenting him with a single-fingered salute.

"Doctor Saturday and co." he read. "Ruddy stupid

name." His eyes flicked back to the cheap piece of electronics.

Could save you a bob or two.

Sucking the last dregs of tar out of his foul-smelling cigarette, he snatched up his duct tape swaddled handset and dialled the number on the business card.

"Doctor Saturday and co." chirped a pleasant female voice. "How may we help you?"

"I was told you could 'elp me with some little thugs who keep vandalising me car."

"Well, doesn't that sound just downright, terrible?" the woman said, her voice brimming over with earnest sincerity. "I'm sure Doctor Saturday would have something right up your street. Please hold while I connect you."

Baldwin sat for a few moments and listened to some soothing music that sounded like whales mating until a deep, masculine voice took up the call. "Doctor Saturday here. How may I help you?"

"Well, it's like this, some little sods keep vandalising me car, don't they? I want them to stop."

"I see," came the reply. "May I take your name?"

"It's Baldwin. Thomas Baldwin."

"Well, Mister Baldwin," Doctor Saturday replied, "I think I might be of service to you. All it would take would be a simple revulsion spell. When the young offenders tried to damage your car, they would be put into a state of *gravi vomitus*, making them unable to…"

"Gravy what?"

"*Gravi vomitus*. Severe vomiting."

Baldwin took a second to process this. "You mean they'd puke their guts up?"

"Eloquently put."

A smile spread across Baldwin's face. "I like the sound of that? 'Ow much?"

"Five thousand pounds."

"Jesus! The car's not even worth 'alf of that."

"Ah, I see. Then perhaps I might suggest a confusion curse?"

"Ooo… A *curse*." If Baldwin hadn't been holding the geriatric handset, he would have been rubbing his hands with glee. "Tell what that one does then."

"Very well," Saturday continued. "Do you have an image of the individuals?"

Baldwin nodded as he glanced at the fuzzy image on the monitor. "Yes, I do."

"Jolly good. All you would need to do would be to send me a copy of that and I would ensure that, whenever the miscreants walked down your street they would enter a state of *confusione maxima* and would forget where they were until they reached their own *familiae domus*."

Baldwin frowned at more words that he didn't understand, but decided that it still sounded like a good idea, so asked, "So, 'ow much for that one?"

"Three thousand."

"Pounds?"

"Well we don't deal in white chickens these days."

"You being funny with me?"

"Certainly not, sir. Am I to assume then that you might like to try something at the bargain end of our range?"

"Damn right I do. I'm not made of money."

"Very good, sir." There was the sound of a keyboard clicking before the good doctor said, "Here we go then, how about *impius voluntate*?"

"What does that do?"

"Something very unpleasant, sir."

Baldwin grunted as, once again, his eyes tried to focus on the fuzzy image of the young vandals. "'Ow much?"

"Five hundred, and this one comes with a twenty-four hour clause."

"What does that mean?"

"If it doesn't work within twenty-four hours, you don't have to pay."

Little wheels that calculated permutations to the slightest penny started to spin frantically in Baldwin's head. "Sounds like my sort of thing," he grinned.

"I thought it might. Now, if you just let me have your email address, I'll ping the relevant documents for you to *signum in linea.*"

"Pardon?"

"Sign on the dotted line."

It was dark, but the image on the monitor was still viewable.

Just.

Baldwin had signed the agreement, scanned it and emailed it straight back. He had received a confirmation within the next hour that the spell had been cast and he was to provide payment the next day, once it had been successful.

As the evening drew on, though, the man's scepticism had grown.

Witch doctor? Ruddy stupid idea. Surely this was just the sort of thing that middle-class yuppies fell for? He'd seen the ads on television. "Got more money than sense? Well you need to buy my latest piece of mumbo-jumbo!"

At least there was the twenty-four-hour clause. When the stupid thing didn't work, he could ring them up and say so. Job done, walk away, no payment.

There was movement in the corner of the screen.

Baldwin leant closer, his roll up of foul tobacco, glued to his damp lips. "There you are, you little scrotes," he glowered as the three fuzzy teenagers swaggered down the alley, baseball bats in hands. He shook his head. What the hell had he been thinking? No hoodoo would stop these little buggers. Only a swift kick up the jacksie. He was just about to get up and administer some one-man justice when he saw something move on the screen. As the youths approached his poor car, swinging their bats in trial manoeuvres, Baldwin noticed that the asphalt seemed to ripple. He hit the top of the cheap monitor, at first thinking it was interference, but the movement came again, this time stronger, and what's more the kids noticed it too. One turned and pointed with his baseball bat.

A bat which was immediately snatched away by a long, twisted tentacle that shot up out of the road.

"Christ!" Baldwin yelled as he lurched up away from the monitor, sending his plastic chair flying.

The reaction from the would-be vandals was similar. They appeared to be shouting as more of the tentacles erupted from the dark, patched road surface. They turned, dropped their weapons and made to flee, but one by one each of them was snatched up by a muscular, suckered appendage. They were flailed around from side to side as if they were made of nothing but cloth before the tentacles dragged them down into the ground.

The sight of the battered and bleeding bodies folding up then squeezing down into the road before the asphalt slid easily back into a place was something that Baldwin thought he would never be able to forget. He dragged a sweaty palm down over his gaping mouth before he jumped up and ran out to the back alley.

It was as if nothing had happened. There was no blood, no body parts. Even the baseball bats had gone. Carefully, he jumped up and down a few times in the middle of the alley. There was no spring, no give. The surface didn't cave in and nothing came up and grabbed him.

Cautiously, he approached his car.

Not a scratch.

Not a single mark.

Yes, it really was as if nothing had actually happened.

The avaricious wheels inside his head began to squeak into action once more. There was no evidence here of the youths ever having visited. The road was intact; all evidence was gone. There was nothing.

Who was to say that the spell had worked?

It was just mumbo-jumbo after all, wasn't it?

A satisfied smile crept across Baldwin's face.

That's right, he thought to himself, *nothing happened, so I don't need to…*

The sensation of something tightening around his leg snapped him out of his grand designs of non-payment of money due. He gasped as he was snatched from his feet and sent sprawling onto his front. Desperately, he clawed at the rippling asphalt with his dirty cracked fingernails, only to find himself slipping down into the dark place where those with wicked intentions were doomed to go.

Little Acts Of Kindness

Barry could not help but smile as he stepped out of his front door. The reason for this was the glorious spring sunshine that greeted him that morning. It had been such a miserable winter. There had been very little snow but it had been so wet and cold. He could not recall a single week from October to March which had not seen at least one day of damp, miserable precipitation. As a result, his elderly joints had ached liked fury. Now though, the sun was out, flowers were blooming and birds were nesting in the trees at the end of the road.

Barry liked birds. As he walked slowly down the road, the white-haired octogenarian listened intently to the wide variety of songs that twittered through the clear air. There was a robin, the jazz musician of the avian world modulating its free form melody every couple of lines in an intricate cascade of improvised notes. There was a blackbird, a calm steady voice of the British hedgerows calling out to its mate which echoed in loving mimicry. There was a bullfinch, its powerful little trilling cutting across all who sang around it like a trumpet picking up a playful line in a soulful sonata.

Yes, birds were the wonders of creation. They brought vibrancy and colour to an otherwise drab existence and complemented a beautiful day, such as this one, with their fetching songs.

They had troubles though, bless their little hearts. Their natural habitats were constantly under threat, being redeveloped into ugly suburban housing. Their hunting grounds were polluted with toxic chemicals that poisoned their food chain. So it was that one had to perform little acts of kindness to help them. Barry had a number of bird boxes in his garden along with feeders and bowls of water in which his feathered visitors could bathe. These were regularly frequented by joyous little guests whom he watched from the comfort of his conservatory through his old pair of Swiss-made binoculars.

As a matter of fact, it was because of his love for all things avian that Barry was wandering into town today. Yesterday, he had been to a delightful little chat at the local Baptist church where a professional ornithologist had been telling the *Young At Heart* group about which water birds they could expect to find gracing the local canal with their presence this summer. As a result, Barry had missed the delivery of a parcel and had found a small red card popped through his letterbox. He slipped his hand inside his jacket pocket just to make sure that he had remembered it. Yes, there it was. Safe and sound.

He was just thinking about how silly he would feel if he was to arrive at the post office without the card when he heard a plaintive crying. Frowning, he looked around to locate the source of the noise. It was a small boy, no more than four, sat under a large lime tree at the end of the road. Barry shook his head. What on earth was a child of that age doing out on his own? Some parents these days had no sense.

The little boy saw him standing looking, sniffed and whimpered, "I've lost my balloon." The four words were filled with such sorrow that Barry felt quite overcome with pity.

"My poor little chap," he replied, stooping as much as his elderly back allowed him to, "where has it gone?"

The small boy pointed a grubby finger up into the tree. Barry followed the extended snot-coated digit and observed a blue ribbon fluttering in the warm breeze of the day. It was not too high up, but obviously out of reach for the little boy.

"Well, let's see what we can do about that, shall we?" Barry smiled. He reached over and tugged gently on the ribbon. It moved with no resistance whatsoever and the balloon, which had only been resting beneath two leafy branches, drifted back down without any dramatic incident.

The small boy's face split wide in a smile as he snatched his beloved toy from Barry and ran away down the road without so much as a thank you.

The elderly gentleman smiled quietly to himself and carried on into town. Just as he was about to cross over the road at the end of the street, he heard an insistent yapping. There, barking at the passing cars was a small terrier. It was white from nose to tail with an irregular pattern of brown splodges running down its back.

It was also likely to get run over.

Carefully, to the accompanying symphony of creaking limbs, Barry crouched down onto his elderly haunches and whistled.

The dog stopped barking and cocked his head to one side as it looked at him.

Barry patted his aching knee. "Come here boy!" he called, smiling encouragingly as he did so.

The errant canine gave up on the passing traffic and padded over to its new friend, who it began to excitedly sniff.

"There, there boy," Barry soothed as he stroked the little dog's back before fiddling with its collar to read the attached name tag. "So you're... *Pudding*, are you?" he mused. "Hmm... Curious name for a dog. Now, Pudding," he managed to turn the small disc over with his arthritic fingers, "let's see if you have an address. Ah, here we are: 5, Talbot Street. Well, you've not gone very far. Let's get you home, shall we?" He reached into a pocket and pulled out a neatly coiled length of string. When he had been a child, his father had always told him to make sure he had two things with him when he left the house: his wits and a decent piece of string, because both would always come in handy on a regular basis. He tied the improvised leash around the dog's collar and led it along to the next street.

Number five was just around the corner: a faded blue door which had not seen a coat of paint in many years. Barry knocked as loud as his tender knuckles would manage without causing too much discomfort and waited patiently until the door was opened by a middle-aged man wearing a stained football strip and a frown.

"What you selling, granddad?" he asked, his eyes not masking his suspicion.

Barry explain politely that he was not, in fact, a disreputable door-to-door salesman but that he was actually returning the man's dog (which was bouncing up and down frantically at his feet).

The man gave a sullen huff, grabbed the dog, said something unsavoury about *bleedin' do-gooders* and slammed the door in Barry's face.

Barry sighed and continued on his journey into town.

A little while later and the post office was almost in sight. He was just making his way up the bland pedestrian precinct when he saw a woman roughly the same age as him staring down at the floor. He followed her eyes and observed that her purse was lying on the scuffed paving stones. She must have dropped it. It was a busy morning and the street was thronged with people hurrying from one shop to another, yet not one of them stopped to help the poor woman.

Barry walked over, picked up the purse and handed it to the fellow pensioner. "There you go," he smiled from under his neat white moustache.

Rather than showing any appreciation, the woman clutched the purse to her chest and backed off, staring at him in abject horror. When she felt that she was far enough away and in no imminent danger from this un-known man, she turned and darted into a nearby shop.

Barry sadly shook his head and continued on to the post office.

There was no queue at the collection point, yet the pensioner had to wait patiently to be served. A young man on duty finally mooched up to the scruffy, unpolished counter in answer to the bell that Barry had rung a few minutes earlier. The elderly gentleman fished into his jacket and pulled out the red slip which he handed over to the sullen youth. The postal worker snatched the scrap of card out of Barry's hand and proceeded to rummage through a stack of haphazardly placed parcels and Jiffy bags. When he finally located the right one, he dumped it with a certain lack of care onto the grubby counter. "Need to sign," he muttered, handing over a handheld device.

Using the proffered stylus, Barry signed for his parcel and passed the electronic device back. "Thank you, young man. Have a lovely day."

"Whatever."

Barry picked up the shoebox-sized package and tucked it under his arm before heading out of the building. Back on the high street, he headed to the nearest coffee shop for a much-needed rest and a little sit down. After a lengthy queue, he took his milky coffee to a corner table and proceeded to inspect the parcel. He was just about to open it when another customer knocked his shoulder. "Look where you're going!" grumbled the man, even though Barry had been sat down and far from mobile.

He just smiled politely and returned his attention to his post as the rude man carried on shoving more coffee drinkers out of his way.

There were, in fact, two boxes inside the package: one large, one small. Barry opened the small one first. It contained a glass vial of clear liquid. He carefully unscrewed the container and sniffed hesitantly before wrinkling his nose in disgust. Quickly tipping the vile contents into his coffee, he vigorously stirred the concoction before downing it all in one. Even the sweetness of the sugar-laden milky brew could not mask the acrid aftertaste of the vial's contents. Needs must, though. Needs must.

Having dealt with the first of the parcel's contents, Barry turned to the second. It was a black box about the size of a small pile of books. There was no way to open it but there was a meshed grill along the top and a green switch on the side. Barry knew exactly what to do. He had received the simple instructions in an email a few days previously. He flicked the switch and placed the anonymous-looking device under the table as a thin, green vapour started to drift lazily up from the grill.

Then, after neatly dabbing his moustache with a paper napkin, he headed home.

A few months later saw the finest summer that Barry could ever remember. From the pleasant coolness of his ventilated conservatory, he sat studying the cornucopia of birds that now hopped and chirped merrily around his back garden whilst he imbibed a relaxing nettle tea that he had brewed previously on his trusty Primus stove. He made a mental note that the crucial piece of apparatus was due a thorough stripping down and a good clean to ensure that it remained in full working order. Yes, it was somewhat inconvenient now that electricity was a rare commodity these days since the *event*; things were rather more labour intensive. However, it had certainly been worth the desperately radical thinning of the herd. Those who had survived, those with the antidote, had all been more than willing to make personal sacrifices in order to help restore the natural balance. Just looking out at the vast array of songbirds in his garden was a testament to the rewards that were now being reaped by the planet.

The plague had been tailored to target only the all-consuming human race. Those creatures unable to defend themselves from the relentless excess of humanity could now live in prosperity and freedom. The people who had consumed the provided antidote now remained to document and maintain the resurgence of the countless lifeforms which humanity had endangered in recent years. Barry had heard all manner of exciting news from around the globe concerning repopulation and reforestation. Information travelled back and forth across a rudimentary radio network and he always listened in with great interest on his solar-powered receiver.

As he leaned forward and watched a baby sparrow hopping around the feeder table after its mother, he felt very proud of his little act of kindness.

Memento

Darting rain stung the apparently young woman's chilled flesh as she hurtled through the dark woods at a speed unimaginable by those who pursued her. Dishevelled long blonde hair clung to her scalp and her neck as she paused briefly to listen to the night. Her hyper-acute senses detected no more than woodland creatures scurrying down into the protective earth to escape the accursed precipitation.

The woman scowled. She hated rain almost as much as she despised those who she had lost by weaving in and out of the trees and shadows of the dense forest. The land where she had spent her formative youth had been far warmer. Hot sun had baked fine sand and the water she had known had been the warm lapping of the Mediterranean at her toes as she had paddled as a child, hunting for shells.

This country, however, was the epitome of wet. It rained almost all the time, and when there was no rain there was the continual reek of mould and effluent.

Did its inhabitants not know how to bathe?

She really had no idea how her partner could have

endured it for so many centuries.

The woman shifted the dead weight on her shoulder as she let her senses roam her surroundings. No, the noises of her pursuers had faded away into the far distance. However, there was something else.

Smoke.

The fragrant aroma of a hearth.

Even with her unusual strength, the woman was tired from carrying her burden, a burden that needed rest and recuperation. What to do? Should she try and find somewhere dry in what appeared to be the wettest place on the gods' earth or should she risk the charity of strangers.

She shifted her load one more time and frowned as her hand came away soaked in blood.

Strangers it would have to be.

If they protested, she could always kill them.

Nathan was a man of simple means. His modest hut in the middle of the woods provided him with the privacy that he required for his art. No one ever visited him because, apart from those who collected his heavier wares, no one could ever find him. If he needed the contact of others for food or for trade, he would climb into his rickety old cart and ride the winding distance to the nearest village. Quietly and conscientiously he tapped at his chisel that was carving out the final touches to his latest work: a misericord for a church somewhere far away. He had no idea where, nor did he care. Men with money paid him well to create things of beauty. His life, he felt was idyllic.

Except for one thing.

Laying his tools down on his bench he peered over

at another misericord which he had yet to start and tugged pensively at his chin. So far, he had completed four and was almost finished on the fifth. The sixth pew seat, however, sat there blankly regarding him in the exact same manner as a sullen hound awaiting some tasty scraps from the table.

He had no idea what to carve upon its wood.

Normally, the designs just presented themselves. He would wake in the morning and there they would be ready in his head as if they had been fermenting like a good ale overnight. He would pick up his tools, go to work and produce an object of serene beauty. This seat, however, was being stubborn. Nothing was coming to mind.

"What am I to do, my friend?" he sighed, turning around to regard his silent companion. The carver eased himself up from his table and approached the huge stone statue that dominated the far end of his workshop. Its empty stone orbs gazed vacantly into the room as Nathan ran an affectionate hand over one of its curled wings. "I don't know," he smiled, "never any advice." Then he chuckled and poured himself a draught of ale from the barrel that rested next to the grotesque. "None of this for you, then." He winked mischievously and was about to taste the drink when there was a hurried knocking at the door. The mason frowned. "Expecting anyone?" he asked his creation.

The statue remained resolutely silent.

"Must be for me then," he muttered as he walked over to the entrance to his cottage.

On opening the door there was an explosion of rain, blonde hair and dishevelled clothing as a young woman fell through the doorway with a companion slung over her shoulder. The stranger turned, glanced at

Nathan, looked as if she were about to say something then promptly passed out on the floor.

The solitary workman looked at the two beautiful women unconscious at his feet and said to his silent companion, "Well that's not something I see every day."

They were coming for her. She could hear their relentless feet crashing through the night.

"Scorpion! Quick, this way!"

She turned and saw her friend, her companion, her creator, her lover, Tigress, beckoning for her to follow, gesturing with an outstretched hand.

Scorpion picked her feet up to follow but it was as if they were mired in mud.

In clay.

She looked down and saw wet viscous hands oozing up out of the ground, slithering up her legs and pulling her down. Desperately, she reached out to her lover but her hands dropped as she saw the redhead slumped down on the floor, blood gushing from her middle.

There was nothing she could do. They had her and they were dragging her down.

The hands methodically inched their way up her back, their clammy fingers prodding and probing as they encompassed her body.

She felt a hand touch her shoulder and gently shake her.

Her blue eyes snapped open and she grabbed the hand in a vice.

There was cursing from its owner.

Scorpion ignored the expletives and quickly scanned her immediate surroundings. It was the cottage that she had seen in the forest. She had carried Tigress here and entered before there had been the dream.

Tigress had been hurt.

Tigress!

She thrust the hand away and its owner clattered to the floor. Scorpion turned to see her lover lying aside her in bed. She appeared peaceful, asleep, but exceptionally pale.

The blonde woman grabbed her friend's shoulders and started to vigorously shake her back and forth. Tigress' head bounced rhythmically up and down on the bedlinen but the redhead did not respond.

"Your friend is gravely hurt," came a voice.

Scorpion spun around and glared at its source.

"Careful, careful. She was like that when you arrived two nights ago."

It was a man, about forty by the looks of him. Light brown hair, a stubbled chin and dark brown eyes that watched her carefully from behind outstretched protective hands that bore workman's callouses on the fingers.

Scorpion inhaled deeply. Aside from smells of woodsmoke, dust, freshly carved timber and stone, there was just flesh and blood. He was human.

Harmless.

For now.

She ignored him and returned her attention to her companion. Softly, the blonde woman ran her fingers down an ice cold cheek. Shaking her head, she lifted the bedding to check on Tigress' wound. What she saw made her gasp. It was not just the ferocity of the deep gash that stretched across her lover's mid-rift but the fact that she was completely naked.

It was then that Scorpion realised that she too was

not wearing a single stitch of clothing.

Nathan watched carefully as the woman realised that someone had removed her clothes. This was not good.

"So, let's not lose our temper now. Your garments were damaged and covered in blood." He spoke quickly as she paced towards him. "I took them off to clean them. Look, they are over there, repaired." He pointed frantically at the pile of clothing on the stool in the corner of the room, causing the woman to halt her murderous advance. She shot the clothes a quick look and stared back at him again before marching over and grabbing her tunic. Nathan felt himself flush as it dropped over her lithe body.

Once dressed, the blonde gave him an awkward little nod before returning to her companion.

"Don't mention it," Nathan managed as his heart rate started to calm back down. He maintained a cautious distance as the woman knelt quietly on the bed and went back to stroking her companion. "She looks very ill. I'm not sure that I can help her any more. I stitched the wound together as best as I could." Slowly, like a man approaching a wild beast that had wandered in to warm itself by his fire, he walked around the bed. Carefully, in order to protect the redhead's modesty, the mason pulled back the bedclothes to reveal his unconventional handiwork. "See, nice and neat, but I think she needs help from the village."

The blonde ran a slender finger over the puckered wound and shook her head, then looked up at Nathan and repeated the gesture once again, this time more assertively.

"But she could die!" he protested.

The corner of the blonde's mouth curled up into a

curious little smile as, once more, her head slowly moved from side to side.

The man was no threat, of that Scorpion was sure. He had taken them both in with no question, cleaned and mended their garments and, bless him, had tried to save Tigress' life.

If only he knew. She could not help but smile.

The wound was savage and definitely needed treating, but not by a mortal quack nor a physician. She looked up at the man again and considered what needed doing. She did not think he would panic, nevertheless she reached out and gently gave his warm hand a quick squeeze before placing a single finger to her lips.

He understood and nodded.

Scorpion nodded back then took her wrist to her mouth and bit down hard. There was a small gasp from the man and she raised her blonde eyebrows at him.

"Sorry," he apologised.

She turned back to Tigress and let the blood from her wrist trickle across her lover's wound. As it did so, she rubbed it into the gash with a finger. Gently, she worked the life-giving liquid back and forth until her own flesh-wound began to heal. Absentmindedly, she licked at her wrist with her tongue, not wasting a drop and, as she did so, Tigress' wound began to writhe under the blood. Scorpion was aware of the man drawing closer and watching open-mouthed as she continued to massage the fluid into Tigress' flesh. Then, when it had all been absorbed, she tugged gently at the crude thread that their saviour had used two nights previous and slowly prised it out, leaving behind fresh, smooth skin.

She looked up at the man and her blue eyes

twinkled in the firelight.

"Marvellous," he gasped from behind a wide smile.

Scorpion grinned back at him.

He leaned in closer and his hand warily approached the smooth, healed skin. "May I?" he asked.

Scorpion nodded as she absentmindedly ran her fingers through the unconscious woman's hair.

The man's hand gently traced a line where only a moment ago a vicious life-threatening wound had cut a deep groove. "Truly amazing. A wondrous thing." His voice was no more than a whisper. "She is so cold." Scorpion smiled to herself as he drew the bedclothes up around her partner. It was not necessary, but again it illustrated his kindness.

There was a loud growling from the man's stomach. "Oh!" he exclaimed. "It appears that I am hungry. Would you like to eat?"

Scorpion gave him another quiet smile.

"Or should that be, *do* you eat?"

The woman's smile widened as she gave him an affirmative nod. True, she did not *need* to eat, but to refuse the kindness of this nice man would be rude. Quietly, she followed him over to a small wooden table. There was just one chair. "I'm not used to entertaining," he explained, offering the battered seat to his unusual guest. "I shall fetch myself a stool."

Scorpion let her eyes gaze around the room. The best word to describe it was *functional*. On one side was the bed, a simple wooden affair with plain linen. Then there was the small table for dining, although, judging by the tools dotted about it, it served as a type of workbench too. Then, past the fire, was the workshop proper. Her keen eyesight flitted from various woodcarvings up to a huge winged beast that resided by the far wall.

The man came back to the table juggling two bowls of something that he had spooned out from a pot on the fire. "You like him?"

Scorpion nodded quickly before tasting the concoction in the bowl. Gods it was vile, but she pretended it was the most delicious thing she had ever tasted so as not to offend her attentive host.

"I was commissioned to carve about a dozen of them for a church somewhere up north," the man explained. "The others have already gone but there wasn't enough room for him on the carts, so they are collecting him next month. It's funny, but I feel that he watches me all the time. Not in a sinister manner but in some sort of curious fashion. I feel that he needs a name, you know? He has a personality. But I just cannot think of what to call him.

"Oh!" he slapped his hand to his forehead. "Where are my manners? I haven't properly introduced myself." He hastily wiped his right hand on his smock before thrusting it out. "I am Nathan. Very pleased to meet you."

Scorpion took his hand and gave it a quick shake, watching his eyes as they felt her skin.

"Your friend is not the only one who is chilled to the bone."

Scorpion shrugged.

"May I enquire as to what *your* name is?"

She placed the bowl of noxious gloop down on the table and rolled up her sleeve to show the tattoo that adorned her shoulder.

Nathan frowned. "What manner of beast is that? It looks like a spider, but it has a tail like a lance."

Scorpion frowned. This was somewhat frustrating.

She mimed for writing implements and Nathan fetched a piece of charcoal and a thin slip of wood. She wrote her name down for him to see and he looked at it as if he was a monkey examining the intricacies of a plough.

"I'm sorry," the carver apologised, "reading is not my strong point. I just carve."

Scorpion let out a long puff of exasperation and looked over her shoulder to her sleeping companion. What she would give for her mouthpiece to be up and about right now!

Three days passed and, as they did, Scorpion started to relax into her new found domestic situation. Nathan was an impeccable host, providing her with a warm bed (which she shared with the still unconscious Tigress), stimulating conversation and less than edible food. Unable to be parted from her lover, she never left the hut but busied herself by studying the skills that the craftsman utilised in his work.

"It's like this," he explained one morning as he whittled away on a small piece of timber, "I feel that I have to create life, you know? I take this inanimate object and, with my hands and tools, I breathe vitality into it. It may not walk or talk, but when people look at it, they can feel it breathe. The hairs stand up on the nape of their neck and they truly believe that my work has a soul. Like that fellow over there," he motioned to the grotesque. "One day, he will stand with his companions above a thriving city and people shall look up, knowing that he watches over them. They will see the stone statue, but they will feel the living, thinking creature."

Scorpion looked over at the statue and she knew exactly what Nathan meant. It really was as if those blank eyes were watching her and taking in every detail.

So it continued until on the fourth morning, shortly after daybreak, an unfamiliar noise crept into the room.

"*Cassie...*"

There was a blonde blur as one moment Scorpion was stood hovering over Nathan's shoulder, then the next she was knelt on the bed holding her lover's cold hand.

"*There you are...*" came the frail voice, "*my beautiful Trojan.*"

The blonde woman pressed the redhead's hand to her mouth and covered it in kisses.

"Missed me?" Tigress' voice gained strength as her green eyes twinkled and she pulled herself up to a sitting position. "Where are..." Her voice trailed off as she spied Nathan hovering in the background.

Scorpion felt her lover's body tense into flight or fight. She cupped a hand around the seated woman's cheek and turned her head upwards. Smiling, she shook her head.

Tigress studied her partner's eyes and began to relax. "He's good?"

Scorpion nodded, her blonde hair falling around her face.

The redhead reached up and tucked a stray hair behind the blonde's ear. "If you say so." Then she turned to their host. "Greetings! I'm Tigress. You got any ale? I feel like a hog has been using my throat for a latrine."

Nathan's paralysis broke as he hurried over with a wooden cup of liquid. "Pleased to meet you. I am Nathan. Your companion brought you here a few days ago. You were gravely ill. She nursed you back to health."

Tigress glugged down the contents of the cup. "Gods, that's good! That's my Scorpion, always dragging me out of danger."

"Scorpion." Nathan felt the texture of the new name roll around his mouth. "That is the creature you have on your arm?" he asked the blonde.

"Sure is," the redhead answered. "And this is me," she pointed to the fierce-looking tattoo on her respective shoulder. "We got two for the price of one some years ago." She chuckled at the perplexed look on the carver's face. "You don't get out much, do you?"

Nathan shrugged. "Nor do I entertain much. Oh! You must be starving. Would you like something to eat?"

Tigress gave Scorpion a curious frown as the blonde chuckled quietly to herself.

It had been so quiet: Nathan thought to himself as he carefully engraved a rose onto the rim of a wooden plate that he had been toying with. When it had been just him and Scorpion, it had felt like not much had changed. Life had more or less carried on as normal. There had been no incessant chatter, no raucous laughter and no random assortment of clothing distributed around his small home. When the two women had arrived, the only clothes they had possessed were the ones in which they had been dressed. However, since Tigress had awoken, there seemed to be random heaps of female clothes appearing around the place. It was as if she mysteriously magicked them out of thin air.

When he asked them what certain articles were, Nathan just nodded politely in complete befuddlement as the excitable redhead listed off long exotic names for items the purpose of which he could not even begin to imagine.

This was not to say that he did not like her. Far from

it. She was more intoxicating than the strongest ale he had ever quaffed. Late into the night, she would tell tales of far off lands where she and Scorpion had stood back to back, battling foes of overwhelming numbers, always to emerge victorious and dripping in the spoils of war.

"I guess we just got over-confident," she admitted one night, idly spinning her wooden cup between her hands. "We thought we were invincible. It almost got us killed."

Nathan watched as Scorpion placed a hand on her partner's wrist and emphatically shook her head.

"I know. I know that's not possible. Not here, not now. We both know how it ends for us," Tigress mused, the weight of the world in her voice. "It's just, it felt so close. Death was snapping at our heels and, as I felt darkness grab me, I began to wonder if what I saw when I was created was wrong. Silly, I know."

"When you were *created*?"

For the first time since she had awoken from her wound, Tigress was still, silent.

"It's okay," Nathan reassured her. "I know that you are not like me, like other people. I have seen you healed from a wound that should have claimed your life. I have seen that you do not leave this hut during the daytime." He smiled, "I have seen you surreptitiously discard your food into the fire. You are not human, are you?"

"No, we're not," Tigress said, the flickering of the fire making her eyes gleam like the finest emeralds. "We were once, just like you. But that was many, many years ago. We have watched empires rise and fall yet we still carry on doing what we do."

"And what would that be?"

The woman's hand subconsciously stroked where

she had been wounded. "Kill those who would see us slaughtered." She looked over at the blonde and unspoken words flew between them before she continued, "There is a war, Nathan, the likes of which you would never imagine. It has been simmering away in the cooking pot of history since certain ingredients were added at the dawn of time and we are just foot soldiers doing our duty. There are creatures out there that look like you and talk like you. They wear your clothes and eat your food, yet they have no soul. They are monstrosities created by some malign force to infiltrate your world and hunt down those which stand against that belief which these monsters hold firm to in their inhuman hearts."

"And what, may I ask, *is* that belief?" the carver inquired.

Tigress looked him squarely in the eyes. "That the human race is an abhorrence and needs to be eradicated and that those which would be its saviours must be located and destroyed."

Nathan sat back on his stool and frowned. "By saviours, do you mean those like you?"

Both of the women slowly shook their heads.

"No," Tigress said, a distant look in her eyes. "Not us. But it is our job to find them." There was a pause and then she said, "But in the meantime, do you have any more of that ale?"

A few days later, a cart rattled down the overgrown path to Nathan's cottage. The carver was busying himself by the fire with a pot of vile-smelling liquid which he explained to his guests was a preservative to be applied to his wooden creations to stop them from rotting.

Tigress peered into the noxious gloop and feigned

vomiting. "You mean that men of the cloth will be perching their pious posteriors on this rancid brew?"

Nathan chuckled. "By the time it dries, it will not smell as bad. By the time they have been installed, there will be no trace of it remaining."

"Shame," Tigress grinned, "it would cover their pompous flatulence."

The two of them were laughing and Scorpion was smiling when there was a hammering at the door.

"Ah!" cried out the craftsman, "Time for our friend to depart." He crossed the room and opened the door. There on the threshold was a rough-looking man of average height.

"Are you the mason?"

"Yes, yes. Come in. Come in."

As the newcomer entered the building, his nose wrinkled. "What is that awful stench?"

"Apparently it's to protect some seats from pious posteriors," Tigress called out.

The man's eyes flicked across the room to the bubbling pot then to the two women stood next to it. He frowned and grunted. "It burns my nose. Where's the statue?" He enquired.

Nathan led him to the grotesque, which had been bound onto a trolley ready to be moved.

"Ugly brute, isn't he?"

Scorpion cast her partner a frown.

Tigress just raised an eyebrow.

"Beauty is what's within us," Nathan said as he helped the rude man wheel the statue out of the room. "It can be found in the smallest and the largest thing."

They grunted and strained as they heaved the dead weight up onto the cart before lashing it down tight.

The carter tossed the mason his payment before peering back into the cottage. "In my opinion, some things are just vile to the core." He climbed up onto his seat, cracked his reins and the cart trundled off into the forest.

Sweat covered Nathan's body and his throat felt infernally tight. He gasped frantically as he woke with a start.

"Careful, careful. Calm down."

His head darted left and right as a cool pair of hands held him and soft words soothed him.

"Calm. Calm. It was a nightmare."

"The beasts!" he wailed when his throat finally loosened. "They burnt the ground! Everywhere. Fire!" Then he felt himself drawn close to a chest and inhaled a sweet female scent as Tigress held him tight.

"It's over. It's over," she soothed. "Just a dream."

He wrapped his arms around her and sobbed into her shoulder like a child that had seen its pet hound killed by a boar. "It was so real. So real." When the man had calmed down, he pulled away and rubbed the back of his hand across his wet eyes. "I am so sorry. What must you think of me?"

"That's okay." The redhead kept a comforting hand on his knee. "Scorp has dreams too, you know? Some of them are, well, quite useful."

Scorpion nodded as she too placed a reassuring hand on the distraught man.

"Useful?"

The women nodded as Tigress explained. "Sometimes she sees the future. When she was younger no one ever believed her - some sort of curse - but now... Well it's gotten us out of quite a few situations."

The carver looked from one of the women to the other, then back again. "I sincerely hope that dream never comes true."

"Want to tell us what it was?"

He screwed up his face trying to recall the nightmare. "I can't remember all of it, but I will never forget the heat. Everywhere was burning! The trees were aflame and the ground was scorched. And there was the most monstrous noise, like denizens of hell calling the damned to their wretched fate. I tried to block my ears but could not protect myself from the horrible sound.

"Then I saw its source. There were two dragons, one red and one black. I think the red one had many heads. They were fighting and, as they did, the ground shook and creatures rose from its depths. They were abhorrent! Their skin was brown like dirt and they had no faces that I could distinguish, just mouths that stretched from one side of their head to the other. As the dragons fought, these creatures turned and advanced on me. I knew they wanted to feast on me..."

He trailed off, the looks of concern on the women's faces drawing him to a halt.

"These are the creatures that you fight, aren't they?"

The silence confirmed that they were.

"Why did I dream that? Why did I see such things? Normally, I dream of things of beauty. When I awake, I carve them into wood or stone. I cannot bring these monstrosities to life!"

"We are so sorry, Nathan." Tigress' voice was very quiet. "We have brought our world into yours." She slipped an arm around her partner and their heads touched sorrowfully. "We will pack our things and leave."

82

Nathan stared at the two curious women in their loving embrace and gasped in realisation. "No! No! You mustn't leave." He scrambled from where he had been sleeping and scurried across to his work tools. "No, not yet, anyways." He grabbed the blank misericord and hefted it up onto his work table before scratching rapidly at its bare surface with a sharp implement.

Tigress gave Scorpion a bemused frown.

Scorpion returned her lover's confusion with a shrug.

For the next few hours, the craftsman was in his own little world and heaven help anyone who interrupted him. He had positioned the misericord in such a manner that neither of his houseguests could see what he was creating. All they observed was the master at work, chiselling, scribing, sanding, occasionally standing back to view his work in progress and muttering to himself. Once, Scorpion took him a cup of ale for refreshment. He impolitely snatched it out of her hand and shooed her away much to the amusement of Tigress, who was reclining on the bed, propped up on her elbow.

Eventually, it was apparent that Nathan had finished. He was lovingly applying some of the vile-smelling preservative to the wood and whistling tunelessly to himself. Then, he stood back, smiled and beckoned for the women to come and view his handiwork. When they did, Scorpion was not the only one who was speechless.

"Well?" he asked with the anxiety of all artists. "What do you think?"

Both of the women flung their arms around him, hugged him and covered his head in kisses.

"My, my," the maestro stammered, "I am guessing that you like it."

"Nathan, it's so beautiful!" Tigress lavished praise on the seat as she let her fingers hover over the intricate carvings, first of Scorpion's face, then her own. "It's so real, so lifelike." There in front of her was an exact repro-duction of the two of them embracing. Also, under the re-spective lovers, were carved delicate representations of a scorpion and a tiger. It was impossible not to feel the love that flowed between the two subjects of the carving. Their wooden simulacra were embracing tenderly and detailed pairs of eyes gazed upon each other with obvious adora-tion.

Scorpion, still hugging Nathan, nodded exuberantly before planting another kiss on his blushing cheek.

The man chuckled quietly. "Well, I guess that's it. I'll go into the village tomorrow and send word for them to be collected. If the buyer is half as pleased as you are, I will be content."

The wagon for the misericords arrived four days later, just after the sun had set. Nathan was applying the finishing touches to a small statue he had been working on. "It's just a little side project," he explained to an attent-ive Scorpion who was curled up next to him as he applied the final coat of paint. "I just wanted to make something for you and Tigress." He smiled as Scorpion's face lit up. "Here. Have a look. Be careful, though. The paint's not yet dry."

The blonde woman leant in close and gasped as Nathan carefully placed the small statue of the Virgin and Child on his table. She turned and beckoned frantically for Tigress to come and see.

"You two have brought so much joy to my solitary life," the carver explained, his paint-smeared hands thoughtfully rubbing his cheek. "I've always lived like a hermit. Never really wanted anything to do with other people, but you two have brought sunshine to my world. So I wanted you to have this. She will protect you on your adventures."

Tigress raised a red eyebrow. "You sound like you want us to leave."

He shook his head. "No. Never. But I know your sort. You have so much adventure in your blood that you will not tarry here much longer. So, see this as a memento of your time spent here. A remembrance of me."

A silence hung in the room as an unspoken conversation passed between the two women.

Eventually, Tigress said, "Nathan, it doesn't have to be that way. You could come with us."

The man was about to reply when there was a loud banging at the door. "Ah, that must be the carter for the misericords." He heaved himself out of his chair and plodded over to the door.

It was the same man as before. The shabby-looking carter crept into the warm room. "I've come for the seats," he grunted, his eyes darting from Nathan to the women. "I've brought help."

There was a shambling clatter as six more men traipsed in and started to remove the carved priest chairs. Engrossed in their beautiful gift, Scorpion and Tigress only paid passing attention to the small talk between Nathan and the men. "I never asked where they were headed."

The carter gave a shrug that could not care less. "Some new church that's been built on a magical spring. Apparently it heals folk, if you believe that sort of thing." He stood by the fire, jabbing absentmindedly at its burning logs with an iron poker. "I just do as I am told."

The last of the misericords was loaded onto the cart. The carter gave a nod to the youngest of his companions who climbed back up behind the horses and eased the wagon away into the wood, leaving his six companions behind.

"Aren't you going with your wagon?" Nathan asked.

The carter stood up, holding the red hot poker. "Actually, we have other business before we leave."

Nathan was aware of a number of things happening at once. There was a curious noise from behind him as if someone was drawing his foot out of a wet marsh, the carter threw the poker onto the nearby bed which immediately caught fire, Scorpion and Tigress had shot across the room and, for some reason, there was a burning pain in his bowels. He looked down and saw a sharp object protruding from his stomach, covered in his blood.

Everything went grey.

The noise of transformation was unmistakable.

Constructs.

They had let their guard down and now would have to fight to save not only their lives, but Nathan's too. As they shot across the room, fangs bared and senses heightened, they saw their gentle friend slump to the floor, a bloody hole in the back of his tunic, a partially transformed construct stood over him.

That was the first one immobilised by the loss of its head.

The two vampires moved faster than the mortal eye could comprehend. They shot from one prey to another. Outnumbered, they may have been, but they were Tigress and Scorpion. Their very names poured dread into those that they hunted. One by one, bodies fell into heaps of limbs and puddles of clay as they were torn apart until, in a few minutes, five of the intruders lay incapacitated and ready for draining.

The carter remained. He stood at the door, his sullen eyes watching them. "Vile beasts," he spat, "Children of Adam and Eve's murderous son. *This* is not for the likes of you." He stashed the statue of the Virgin and Child in his jacket. "I shall put it where it rightfully belongs."

Tigress was about to leap at him when a groan came from behind.

"Yes," the carter mused, "you can try to kill me or you can save him who sheltered you all this time. The choice is yours."

The flames from the bed had already spread to the thin walls of the cottage and were starting to consume the carver's wooden creations. The vampires stood tense, desperately wanting to suck the false life out of this creature who had brought suffering to their lives, but Nathan...

"I thought so." The carter turned quickly and left the women with the bodies of his men in the growing inferno.

They needed no words. As one, the two women grabbed the gentle artist and heaved him out of the blazing cottage. The dismembered constructs would have to be left to the heat of the fire. Outside, there was no sight of the carter, nor did they expect there to be. He had disappeared into the forest and the smell of the burning building masked his vile, earthy stench.

They carried Nathan to a clear patch of grass and cradled him in their arms. Scorpion looked desperately from his deep wound to the face of her partner. Tigress looked back and nodded. "Nathan! Nathan, can you hear me?"

The dying man reached up and stroked her cold cheek. "As clearly as ever I could, my sweet Tigress, although all around me grows faint."

A drop of blood that was not his dripped onto his tunic. Tigress looked up and saw that Scorpion was crying. "You don't have to die," she said to her erstwhile saviour. "There is a way that we can save you. You can come with us.

"But it should be your choice."

A weak hand stroked feebly at her face. "No. I am finished."

More blood fell onto his torn body. This time the tears were not Scorpion's. "No, no, no..." Tigress cried, "Please. Don't. You can't. Please. Let us save you. You will be able to make beautiful things forever. Imagine that."

There was a harsh gurgle from the cooling man as he actually laughed. "That could never be, my friends. I have completed my most beautiful works and you have already completed me." His hand slowly fell from her cheek and his eyes stared off into the distance.

Tigress knelt, covered in the blood of one that she had not slain, and words failed her. She was as mute as her lover and companion who knelt with her in the deep forest, illuminated only by the burning building where they had spent a brief, wonderful time with this sweet man in his final days.

They would carry his kindness as a memento in their hearts, until the final day when they knew that their long lives would ultimately end.

They would remember him.

Author's Notes

Thank you for sticking around to the end of this, my fourth collection of short stories. As a little way of saying, "Thank you," I would just like to share a few thoughts and facts about the tales that you have just read.

Orion's Child.

This story and *Here There Be Dragons* are both heavily linked to the world of my investigator of the paranormal, Sam Spallucci. Like the vampire short stories from previous anthologies that focussed on Justice and his children, they will both run for a while before linking in to the main body of Sam's world. *Orion's Child* is the first of a two-parter bringing you, the reader, up to date with what the Bloodline of Abel have been up to since Sam fed the Werewolf of Williamson Park to a host of driver ants. Chris Dootson's anonymous attacker has actually been referenced a couple of times in *Shadows of Lancaster* and *Dark Justice*. If any of you think you have worked out who he might be, feel free to share your theories on social media.

This antagonist, and the unfortunate star gazer

(who is actually based on a real-life stargazing aerial re-pair-man), will return in the second of the stories along with someone exceedingly influential from Sam's past. Watch this space.

Somebody's Gotta Do It.

I have a passion for pre-school books. Especially those which have a quirkiness or hidden darkness about them. These are the ones that not only entertain the child but also make the adult alternately chuckle and squirm. One such story is *Fred-Under-The-Bed* by Nicola Baxter. It is a very short bedtime story about a pair of children who discover a sock monster in their bedroom. Fred has a nasty streak and threatens to eat their teddy bears. I had the thought one day that perhaps the kids might push him too far and he wouldn't just stop at cuddly toys.

Why not read this story to *your* children at bedtime? I'm sure they'd love it!

Frank's Castle.

Lancaster Castle was the inspiration for this very short, very dark tale. A place of imprisonment and torture for many years, I wondered what would happen if someone truly psychotic was to buy such a building. I liked playing around with the style of the story, keeping it very much in the present tense, to give the feeling that you the reader were in fact listening to the poor reporter's demise live on radio.

Not-So-Lucky-Larson.

A little side accompaniment to *Sam Spallucci: Ghosts From The Past*, this story came to me when I was walking home from town earlier this year and was more or less fully formed by the time I had put my key in my front door.

Ghosts took an exceptionally long time to write compared to its predecessor *Casebook* and the whole notion of Malcolm Wallace being a focal point in so many people's lives was something which never really left my mind. There have been a few obvious references in Sam Spallucci's world as to how things have changed after the cult leader's demise, the loss of Caroline from Sam's life to be but one, but I wanted to see if Wallace being erased from history could have an even more profound effect on those who had no knowledge of his darker side.

The third season of *Fargo* was somewhat of an influence here. The police officer, Gloria Burgle, is constantly unable to interact with automated mechanical devices and I wondered at one point, whilst watching the show, if she was actually real. This developed in *Larson* as the unfortunate Nick's life rapidly unravelled and he was eventually obliterated.

Here There Be Dragons.

Like I mentioned earlier, *Here There Be Dragons* is the first of a run of shorts over the next few anthologies. I don't want to say too much here because I could very easily slip into spoiler-hood, especially regarding Kanor. All I *will* say is, pay careful attention to who is doing what in this short story and you might want to go back and re-read a certain barbecue scene in *Sam Spallucci: Dark Justice* then also check certain news items that Sam watches on television.

This little arc is definitely here for the long game.

TV Dinner.

I love writing stories as short as possible. This dark little ditty has been the shortest so far. I hope you enjoyed it.

Wicked Intentions.

This story was written in just a few hours as a way of venting my spleen when some little scrote decided to smash the side window of my new car that had only been driven off the forecourt a few weeks previous.

Unlike Baldwin, I stuck to getting the window fixed and never called on the services of a witch doctor.

Honest...

Little Acts of Kindness.

This story was actually written back in 2016 and was intended to go in *Let All Mortal Flesh*. However, I was not entirely happy with it so, along with another story entitled *The Day The Alien Came*, it was shelved for the time being.

I came back to it this year and tidied up a few things, including the ending, and the final result pleased me so I published it. *Alien* is still languishing in a folder on my laptop. Perhaps it will be good enough next time.

Memento.

I have said it before and I will no doubt say it over and over again, I love Scorpion and Tigress to bits. I felt that they shone in *Sam Spallucci: Dark Justice*, giving a real contrast to the other vampires who were very much still in their infancy compared to these two who had been around the block numerous times. They are full of life, tales and very colourful history, part of which is revealed in this story. More will unfold at a later date when I look at both of their birth stories.

Memento was another one that did not make it into *Let All Mortal Flesh*. This was through no fault of its own aside from the fact that it was just too long for the anthology, so it had to wait. I also think that it works well reading the story after it has been mentioned in *Dark Justice.* It's also an arc which will be revisited quite a bit later on in *Fallen Angel* when all the various threads regarding vamps, angels, Sam and Lucifer are tied up together.

So, I hope you found those ramblings interesting. As always, let me know via social media what you felt about the anthology. This can be theories, likes, dislikes or even just a picture of you reading the book. It's just nice to know my stories are being read.

ASC September 2018.

About The Author

A.S.Chambers resides in Lancaster, England. He lives a fairly simple life of walking in the countryside, gazing at mountains and wondering if clouds taste of candy-floss.

He is quite happy for, and in fact would encourage, you to follow him on Facebook, Instagram X, TikTok, Patreon and YouTube.

There is also a nice, shiny website:
www.aschambers.co.uk

Milton Keynes UK
Ingram Content Group UK Ltd.
UKHW021555270524
443319UK00001B/30

9 781915 679413